just like a

caucasian

ODERA O'GONUWE

First published in the USA by Delu Press.

Copyright © Odera O'Gonuwe 2017

Delu Press
delu.press@gmail.com

ISBN: 978-0-9970766-2-2 (Paperback)
ISBN: 978-0-9970766-3-9 (Ebook)
Library of Congress Number: 2017904875

This book is a work of fiction. Names, characters, places, and incidents are either a product of the author's imagination or are used fictitiously. Any resemblance to actual people living or dead, events, or locales is entirely coincidental.

Printed and bound by CreateSpace, an Amazon company.

Author's Notes

I was twelve when Trayvon Martin was murdered. It was February, and I was in eventh grade.

I remember sitting in front of the television as I waited for my bus and hearing the news for the first time. A seventeen-year-old African American boy from Florida had been killed. Everyone had an opinion, but what I couldn't understand was why Trayvon had to die. In the following months, more and more stories began to pop up in the media with unarmed black men shot by police or civilians. Tamir Rice. Michael Brown.

I became aware of how American society views black boys as older and aggressive, and I wondered why the media always chose a mugshot to portray the victim. And why, I questioned, why did these boys and men have to be shot so many times? It wasn't just once. Six. Ten. Twelve times.

To many people, the police brutality was a shock. What I came to realize was that the senseless murder of black men and women has been going on for a very long time. It only filtered into mainstream America recently.

Just Like A Caucasian is an exploratory novel—for me—and hopefully for you. It's not about taking sides and assigning blame. My purpose is to speak truthfully on racism and how it affects minority youth.

Acknowledgments

My number one supporter is—and always will be—my sister. I wrote the words, but it was her careful critique and helpful input that made this novel a success. Thank you, Ifeoma, for being the one I can always depend on.

I am grateful to my parents and grandma for their belief in me and their unwavering support. Fay Feghali was also an incredible help to me. Thank you for spending the time to talk to me about your experiences as a Christian Lebanese-American. Your contribution is immeasurable.

I would also like to acknowledge Braden Miller (Joanne The Scammer) for coining the phrase Just Like A Caucasian.

Mohammed Wallace

My neighborhood was the definition of pristine. The fresh, green lawns were cut precisely two inches above ground level by Garcia Lawn Services. The two willow trees at the edge of our property were properly trimmed and maintained as per the town's request. Mine was the only house with red bricks, but it shared the same tall, imposing build and poetic symmetry as every other multi-story house in my neighborhood.

The combination wrought the intended effect. Grover Hills screamed clean and expensive. To people of color, it shouted, 'not for sale'.

The white picket fences only added to the aesthetic, really elevating the sales value. Funny how it wasn't until we moved in that my gracious white neighbors put theirs up.

As my ride pulled up to the curb, I raised my hand to salute Mrs. Fielding. She was our closest neighbor on our right, and even though we'd never spoken I'd always felt an undeniable connection to her. Every time I was outside, I felt her beady eyes tracking me. I imagined her standing in her kitchen, the phone always in reach ready to dial 911 on the black boy when he eventually acted up.

Last Christmas, I sent her a back brace... "because I care," I signed. All those hours standing on her feet couldn't be good for her arthritis.

I jumped into the passenger seat, quick to blow a kiss to Mrs. Fielding. Her curtain snapped close, as the sleek convertible pulled away.

"Must you antagonize your neighbors?" Ndidi asked as she checked her reflection in the mirror, rubbing the lipstick smudge off her teeth.

"Antagonism would be telling her that not only am I black, I am also gay."

"As if the two were mutually exclusive," she says, flashing her dimples.

Solid, gold rings decorated her fingers as they curled around the wheel. Ndidi exited Grover Hills with a smooth turn, singing along to the synthetic drone of DJ Fuze's Top 40.

Ndidi's baby blue Bentley cruised through Thornwood, Ohio, passing the heavy belt of American consumption. Thornwood Mall was a hulking metropolis with slots of paved parking lots for the movie theatre, three restaurants, two fast food chains, and the ten story department store. As she drove, the speedometer exceeded the 65 miles per hour speed limit.

"Watch the police give a ticket to your reckless ass."

Her foot stepped on the pedal as she bopped to the repetitive beat of EDM. "I wish a nigga would."

She bent to rummage through the glove box. Her focus slipped as she reached deep into the compartment. I grabbed the wheel, jerking left to avoid the Volkswagen on the other side. She waved away my hand and commandeered the steering wheel, an energy bar in her mouth.

I relaxed in my seat, my heart calming as she slowed her speed. "Ndidi, you don't deserve that license."

"John seemed to think I did."

"John is severely deluded."

"If you have a problem with how I drive, you could always find another chauffeur. Anyway, he said that my accent's cute."

"Yeah?"

"Just before he passed me his number." John. I remembered him. Blond hair, blue eyes, cute in that basic white boy way. He was older than us, a junior in college.

"You guys talking?"

"No, I trashed his number."

"Why?"

"I had no serious intention of ever contacting him, but it wasn't until he said, 'I've always wanted to date a black girl,' that he was dead to me."

"No..."

"Yes."

"He said that?"

"Yes."

"Typical."

Ndidi nodded. "Piteously so."

Ndidi Ikemba

I never thought about moving to America. Though I was born in New York, I never desired to return to my birthplace. I was excited to enter Primary 1 with my friends, Adetola Adekunle and Helen Ogazi. Life in Nigeria sustained me. Everything I knew and held dear was encompassed within the bubble of Lagos Island. Our estate was a social scene. On weekends, we held state dinners with senators and *Nna*'s Japanese business partners. I joined our Edo maid, Grace, to the market, learning Pidgin English and how to barter the best prices. Late at night, my brothers and I would play football with the mosquitoes, passing the ball to each other within the perimeter of our compound. Chelsea vs Manchester United.

Life was good. I was happy...too easily blindsided by *Nna*'s news. He returned home from a six week business trip with many presents, including American passports.

Three months and a 13 million Naira deposit later, we rented our estate to my auntie and her family and sent most of our clothes and toys to the Little Saints Orphanage. After dropping us at the airport, our driver, Musa, steered the Mercedes Benz to our former home. It was to be a present for my cousin's eighteenth birthday.

Arinze, Somto, and I kept silent as *Nna* repeatedly

bribed security with bundles of 1000 Naira notes, and as we hefted our bags onto the conveyor belt, we prayed that God would keep them safe from thieves. We bolted the five suitcases with locks and wrapped them with saran wrap for added security. *Nna* directed us to the terminal, instructing us to keep our heads down and mouths shut. No one wanted an altercation with custom officers. The tension within my siblings and me stayed with us for the duration of the flight, never abating until the plane touched John Glenn Columbus International Airport.

Nne raised the window for the first time. "*Nee anya*, Ndidi," she said. Look. "Remember this moment. This is when we came to America. *Chi di mma*," God is good. I heard her whisper.

"When will we return home?"

"Not for a very long time."

I stepped down the airplane, my legs shaky from disuse. Everywhere around me, I felt assaulted by change. The people looked so different. The air didn't smell as sweet. Lights and glittery signs haunted me from all sides. It was September, and I was cold. My tiny body shivered under my sparkle jeans and purple sweatshirt. I clung to my *nne*, seeking her familiarity and warmth.

The lights were blinding. My feet were pinched. And hunger rumbled in my belly. I didn't voice my discomfort. The armed oyibo men in their uniform of blue reminded me of all I'd been told of the greedy, British colonizers by my grandma. I blocked the pain, making myself small in an effort to disappear into my *nne*'s traditional dress. The last discomfort came upon me. I had a sudden urge to pee. *Nne* carried me to the bathroom, locking me into the biggest stall with her. I remember her remarking on the cleanliness, before pulling my pants down, so that I could relieve myself.

As we washed our hands, *Nne* played with the soap, peppering the foamy bubbles on my face. When I laughed, she said, "You will find joy in America, Ndidi." Her solemn eyes confirmed this. "In Jesus name, amen."

The door opened and a small, oyibo woman bust in. When she saw my *nne* wiping my face with the paper towels, she touched her hand to her face and squealed.

"I just love your outfit, ma'am. Are you African?"

Nne nodded to me, as if to say, 'See, these people can be nice, too.' "Yes, we've just arrived."

"Oh, your English is already so good. I'm traveling to France, myself. Is this your daughter? She's simply darling." Bending to my level, she said, "You must be so happy to be in America. This is the land of the free, you know."

Standing, she shook hands with *Nne* and said in a gracious tone, "Now that I've met you, I have to travel to Africa. I hear such great things about your country."

She smiled and waved, and then disappeared into a stall. With the bang of the door, a sense of finality washed over me. My life before then was gone. Everything—my friends, the parties, the food, the people, even the things I swore I hated—were gone. We were separated by 9400 kilometers.

On my first day in America, an oyibo lady made me burst into tears in the airport bathroom.

Michael Abboud

I still couldn't get used to the feeling of my teeth. After four years of braces, complete liberation felt amazing. For the past three days, I'd been gorging on popcorn and gummy bears. There was a packet of gummies in my pocket. I wasn't hungry, but I felt the need to consume the whole thing. I hesitated because I didn't want to be labeled the weird guy who ate food from his pocket. I mean, it was only the first day.

There were two other people in the room. The woman leaned against the wall. The girl sat with me on the circular table. We took up two of the five seats. I kept my eyes staring blandly across from me while my hand reached into my pocket and made contact with the crisp edge.

"Name?"

The voice come from nowhere; it startled me. "What?"

The girl looked at me like I was the biggest fool on earth. What was her problem?

"She's asking for your name."

"Oh, it's Michael. Michael Abboud."

She rolled her eyes. "I don't want it. She does." She motioned toward the woman standing hesitantly in front of the room.

The woman stashed her phone in her jeans. "Hi,

7

I'm Rose. Sorry for the silence, I had to get some things done, but since it's getting close to the hour, I want to confirm your names, spelling, and potential nicknames. You said Michael Abboud, right?"

She pulled a notepad, flipped it to a blank page, and uncapped her pen. When she finished writing, she listed off the letters. I nodded. The spelling was perfect.

"Great." She turned toward the clock hanging next to the door. "Well, it's after one and although the other two haven't made it, I think we should start." She nudged her pen behind her ear, leaving her notepad on the table. "Let me tell you about myself. As I've said, my name is R—"

The door burst open, and the missing two poured in. They held Starbucks in their hands and a guilty expression crossed their faces. They slid into the remaining seats after closing the door.

"As I was saying, I'm Rose Thompson. I graduated from Ohio State University in 2015 with a major in film. I put together this group to make a documentary and write an accompanying essay about race through the eyes of young minorities. Throughout the summer, we'll have weekly discussions that I'll be recording." She pulled out a black recorder from her purse, flicked it on, and set it on the table. "And I'll be contacting you guys to schedule your individual video tapings. Now, I still need a permission slip from both of you." She glanced at the latecomers.

"Can you get them to me by next week? Today's an information session, but you can't fully participate until I have the paper signed by a parent or guardian. I have extra copies if needed. Now, we'll start by sharing our names—and if you two can provide spelling—that would be great."

The girl to my right stood. "My name is Bianca Villamayor," she said, and then promptly sat back down.

I slicked my hair back before rising. "Hi, I'm Michael Abboud." But that seemed too blunt, so I added, "Nice to meet you," and a little wave.

The other two didn't stand. "Good morning. I'm Ndidi Ikemba." She repeated the spelling for Rose's benefit.

"And I'm Mohammed Wallace."

Rose clapped her hands. "Now that we know each other, and I've told you everything, you're free to leave. Remember, we'll meet again next Saturday, same time, same place."

Ndidi and Mohammed jumped to the door as soon as Rose stopped talking. I turned to Bianca. "So...what made you want to participate in a docu—?"

"I have a boyfriend." She got up to leave.

"Duly noted." I exhaled sharply. It would be only seven weeks. Time flies by so quickly, I'd blink and the end of summer would be near.

Bianca Villamayor

I was mean to that kid, Michael, but I couldn't help it. I hate small talk.

I wish I were getting paid, or at least compensated for the gas expense. My dad's 2001 Toyota Tundra consumed more gas than the trip was worth. When I saw a flyer advertising this program nailed to a tree, I was immediately drawn to it. I screenshotted the phone number and called it during my work break.

Spending the summer investigating racial relations through the eyes of minorities. That sounded smart—smart enough to compensate for being a high school dropout. I needed something to fill my time. The less hours I spent at home, the better.

Michael Abboud

"How did it go?"

"Fine, Mom."

"How do you feel about Rose? Do you like her?"

"She's okay."

"I just got off the phone with her. I've set your individual videotaping with her on Thursday at 12."

"I don't need you to make appointments for me."

"You weren't going to do it. What's your deal?"

I grabbed a drink from the refrigerator. "Who taught you that phrase?"

"My university students keep me updated. My TA set up a Twitter account for me. I tried to follow you, but I was blocked."

I popped the can and took a swig. I forgot how good it was to drink pop straight from the can. "I can't have *my mother* follow me on Twitter."

"Why do you say 'my mother' like that, like it's a curse or something?"

"Nothing personal. It's the principle of it. You know I love you."

"I do, but why don't you like Rose?" she persisted.

"I don't dislike her." I set my Coke down. "I don't have

anything against her."

"But..."

"I don't understand the whole idea of a race documentary."

"What don't you understand?"

"I just think it's ... unnecessary."

"What do you mean?"

"How does this help? We go there and talk about our experiences, and we all know that our stories are going to be full of racism and xenophobia because this is 'Merica."

"This is why Rose is making the documentary, to shed light on this issue. Awareness is the first step in the fight for equality."

"We've been talking about the -isms and -phobias since forever. It's 2017. As of today, if you don't know what's going on in the modern world, *you* are part of the problem."

"So say that in the documentary. Speak for yourself."

"Who's listening to me, an Arab boy? They think I'm a terrorist, remember?"

"Times are changing, Michael. People are starting to understand."

"Nothing has changed. *Nothing*. I live my life with these people. They're my teachers, my classmates, my friends. I hear every negative comment they make against people who look like us. I don't need a documentary or a group meeting to understand that America is as racist as it has always been, and it will probably never change."

"Michael..."

"You act like I'm not speaking the truth. They see my last name and they want to deport me. They don't believe that I—as an American—am deserving of the same rights as them. You know I speak the truth. Remember the hateful messages students would email you, or the extra attention we get from TSA when we fly. They don't want to give me a chance, so why are you asking me to do this for them?"

"You have so much anger inside you."

"You can't tell me I'm wrong because you know I'm right."

"I just wish you had peace."

"And I wish no one discriminated against us."

Bianca Villamayor

I was the first to arrive, but I didn't mind. The building was locked, so when I parked my car, I laid on the grass, waiting for everyone to arrive. Sunlight poured in through the nebulous clouds. A warm glow illuminated my skin. It was the best kind of light, a photographer's dream.

A dated Chevy rolled into the car lot. Rose tripped as she climbed out, almost dropping her coffee, and banging her leg against the side. I heard the expletive as it flew from her mouth.

I thought about waving to her, but only for a second. I closed my eyes instead, leaned back, and pretended to be asleep.

Ndidi Ikemba

Rose sat in her chair, her fingers raised over her keyboard. Three minutes ago, she greeted the group and told us to let the conversation flow freely among us. It would make us more comfortable with each other, she said, as long as we kept in mind our greater theme of race.

No one seemed inclined to say much of anything, so I began. "My parents moved us to America so we could escape changing Nigerian politics and get better opportunities. The opportunities are great, but the culture made it very hard to acclimate."

"My parents say the same. They moved here from Lebanon," Michael said.

And then silence. I felt like I'd done my part, so I sipped my caramel frappuccino. Eventually, all eyes gravitated toward Rose.

"I'm only here as a passive audience. The purpose for this exercise is for you guys to establish your own narratives."

"I hear immigration is hard," Bianca offered.

"What's hard is the disillusionment. It's a very different America that's shown in Hollywood blockbusters than it is in real life."

"My parents thought this was the dreamland," Michael

15

said. "Turns out that there's corruption here just like everywhere else."

"I think corruption is a trait of humanity. Once a society gets big enough, it's like *whoomp there it is*. The only thing America does better is hide it," Mohammed said.

"The West in general likes to claim that it has gotten where it is by sheer ingenuity."

Mohammed interrupted me. "What's not innovative about stealing land from Native people enslaving, infecting, and murdering them in order to fill your coffers back home?"

"Exactly the point I was making. It's easy to claim superiority while completely subjugating everyone else."

"It reeks of inferiority," Bianca said, "If they really were superior, then they'd win on equal standing."

Rose spoke. "Who's they?"

"At first it was the British Anglo-Saxons when they first came to establish the colonies," Bianca said.

"The first illegals," Mohammed added.

"Of course." Bianca continued, "Now, it's the White Americans. Not all, but most."

"Enough to make it a problem," I said.

"Michael, do you have anything to add?"

He shook his head.

"Try harder," she said softly.

"It's all been said. Corruption is alive and well. America isn't as united as it seems to be."

"The only thing that unifies this country is an opportunity

to hate and exclude," Ndidi said.

"Slavery, Islamophobia, the Chinese Exclusion Act. History doesn't lie, but our history books do," Bianca said. "I barely remember covering Japanese Internment in school or the Trail of Tears."

"And we're back to where we started. Racism and xenophobia has been embedded within the fabric of American culture for years. What does our saying it change?" Michael asked.

We looked at one another.

"I don't know," I said.

Bianca Villamayor

I hate conforming to the stereotype above all things, which is ironic considering my family owns a Mexican restaurant. We moved here from California eleven years ago to bring spice and flavor to Ohio.

"*Mija*," my father greeted me.

"*Hola, papá*."

After wading into the apartment, I slipped off my shoes, leaned in and kissed him on the cheek. "How was your day?"

"Busy," he responded, "but good."

My sister exited the bathroom, attired in her uniform, ready for work. She tossed me my shirt. It was black with white lettering that printed, '*Casa de Villamayor*.'

"Is this the new design?"

She nodded. "Classy and chic. I think the black and white really adds to our sophistication."

I rolled my eyes and checked the size. "Why is this an extra small?"

"You've lost so much weight since you had the flu, and baggy shirts don't make you look good. Anyway, I'm heading downstairs to start my shift with Mom. Change quickly, please. We have a lot of customers."

"I'm the older sister, you know. It's supposed to be

me telling you to do things." She only smiled before heading out. I gripped my T-shirt, walking toward my room to change when my father called my name.

"You have mail." He handed me a state-issued document. The top was already torn open. "It took me a while to realize that it was addressed to you," he explained.

I pulled out the certificate. "The state of Ohio now recognizes my high school equivalency." I already passed my GED. This was simply a physical confirmation, but I couldn't help the grin from spreading across my face.

He motioned me toward the light. "Here. Let me take a picture."

I held the certificate in front of me, a cheesy smile plastered on my face.

"I'm so proud of you. I only wish you could have graduated with your peers. Instead of—"

"Leaving home at sixteen."

"I was going to say pursuing a modelling career." He shook his head. "But that doesn't matter. What's important is that you've finished and now you'll go to college like you were always meant to do."

"Why did you do that? Why do you always have to bring it up? Isn't it enough that I came back? You were right, and I was wrong. No one wanted to hire *una Mexicana morena*. Are you happy?"

"I'm just happy you're finally getting your life back on track," he sighed.

"This was supposed to be a celebratory event. Thank you, Papá, for ruining that."

Ndidi Ikemba

I stared at the blinking cursor of my computer screen. The small dash stopped just short of my title. I clicked enter twice and then tab, settling my finger over the keyboard. The idea was there, a glimmer of the future of what my blog could become...I was very good at that, visualizing long-term success.

Twenty minutes later, I still only had my name, date, and the title. For months, I had been fantasizing about this blog, thinking that when I finally started, my fingers would dart across the screen, forming sentences before I'd even thought of them. It would be an eloquent, sharp, witty commentary about... *something*.

I refilled my cup with water, tapping my foot against the marble tiles as I waited for the liquid to reach the brim. If I had my way, I could have been relaxing on Miami Beach after a long day of interning. Two weeks before my flight, I was already packed and ready to leave. And then I got an email informing me the company had shut down and all the employees had been laid off.

I felt the pain of the working class, and it sucked.

I had to scramble to find another program to fill my summer. Thank God I found Rose's project and was able to convince Mohammed to do it with me.

"Damnit."

Water overfilled the cup, spilled across my hand and onto the floor. I slurped the excess water and moved to locate a rag when the doorbell rang.

I padded toward the foyer and unlocked the door. My brother leaned against the frame with aviator sunglasses and a yellow and red multicolored dashiki.

"Somto, *kedu k'ime*?"

"Good. Very good." He folded me into a hug. "How are you?"

"I'm fine. Why aren't you at school, and what happened to your key?"

"I'm in town for a conference and thought I'd stop by and surprise my sister." He squeezed my cheek. "I forgot my key, but now that I'm here, I'll take you out for dinner."

"Let me grab my purse." I dashed upstairs, throwing my phone, wallet, and ID into my bright red tote. After slipping on my sandals, I closed my computer and headed outside where I saw my brother pulling on a black sweatshirt and covering his head with the hoodie.

"You're not wearing that are you?"

"Do you like it? It's new." He posed, slipping his Aviator's down his nose and gifting me with a wink.

"Take it off. These *ndi ocha* call the police first and ask questions when you're dead."

He laughed. "My pessimistic sister. Times are good these days. You hardly hear stories like that anymore."

"Don't say I didn't warn you."

Michael Abboud

Rose had me sit on the chair across from her so that my profile faced the camera. My mom reached behind my back to adjust my collar, and then settled her hand on my shoulder. "I'll be out for a few hours to run some errands. Do you need anything else, Rose?"

"No, Mrs. Abboud. We're fine."

Mom looked smug as she left the living room, because she was getting exactly what she wanted. Her favorite student and her only son were submitting to her gentle prodding. First to make her little race video and then to make me participate in it. I crossed my arms, slouching on the couch.

"What am I supposed to talk about?"

"Let's start with why you're here." She positioned herself behind the camera.

I tapped my foot against the carpet. Already my body felt cramped in my position. Looking into the camera, I said, "I guess this is a documentary about being a minority in America, in my case, an Arab kid in America."

Rose nodded. "That's good. Keep going."

"What else should I say?"

"Explain what it means to be an Arab minority."

"I'm Lebanese. My parents came here before I was

22

born to escape the Civil War. They were one of the lucky ones."

"Go on." When I was silent, she said, "How has your background shaped you into who you are today?"

"I'm grateful to them for all the sacrifices that they've made. Most children of immigrants feel the same way."

"This isn't about other people, Michael. This is about you and your story."

"I'm sixteen, Rose. I don't have a story."

She turned the camera away. "Do you want me to leave?"

"What? No!" *Only because my mom would be very pissed.*

"Because I can. There are many other ways I'd like to spend my Thursdays, and if you want to be taken off the project, all you have to do is say so."

"I do want to be a part of this." *Because my mom said I had to.*

"Then, say something meaningful. I don't want generic answers. I want the truth. I want to know you."

"I don't know where to start."

"Start with your name."

"Michael Abboud."

"Describe yourself."

"I'm a normal guy. I like watching television and playing Halo. I procrastinate like everyone else. I don't always do what I should, but I think I'm a good kid. I try to be respectful and get good grades. Like I said—normal."
I looked at her, waiting for her input, but her eyes were

hidden behind the camera.

"But other people don't see me this way, and I'm coming to realize that other people's perception of you—*of me*—carries a lot of weight."

She spoke now. "And what do other people think of you."

"They see me and see Arab and to them, that means evil."

"How does this make you feel?"

"When I was a kid, I felt guilty. There was this overwhelming sense within me that I was at fault. I'm allowed to share a story, right?"

"You're allowed to talk about whatever you want."

"I first learned about 9/11 in third grade. For the anniversary, my teacher put on an hour and a half long video. I don't know whose bright idea that was, but at the end the movie, he had a classroom of thirty-one bawling eight-year-olds. For weeks, I couldn't get that image of the Towers falling out of my head, and those people...just diving out the building...it was horrific."

"After the video, this kid, Aaron Whitaker yelled from across the room, asking me, 'Isn't your family from the same place as those guys on the movie?' The room was silent for what seemed like forever. No one even sniffled; it was like they were all waiting for my response. Maybe I'm being dramatic, but it seemed like even my teacher, Mr. Mahoney, was waiting for me to speak."

"Until then, I never associated terrorism with people who look like me, and I felt so guilty. I wasn't there. I wasn't even born there, and it was like I was taking all the heat for something I had just learned about. My face was so red and dried tears were all over my face, but I responded to Aaron, saying, 'No, my family's Greek.'"

"The previous weekend, my mom rented *My Big Fat Greek Wedding*, so it was the first thing that popped into my mind. Whenever I tell this story, people always look at me funny and ask why did I lie. They usually follow this up with a speech about the importance of being proud of who you are. But they weren't there in my classroom when Sophie Scholl said, 'Good, I hate Arabs,' and the rest of the class agreed. Not even Mr. Mahoney said a word, and I knew he knew where I was from because he met my parents on Parent Teacher Conference Day."

"Do you blame your classmates?"

"No, I don't blame them. I mean, we were all so young. Living in America, we knew there was a war going on, but we didn't understand it. All we knew was that we were on the attack and that the other side was filled with bad people. When Sophie said she hated Arabs, that didn't come from her. It sounded like an adult speaking through a child. None of them even knew what Arab was. *Aladdin* was their only exposure to that part of the world. I can't blame them for something they were ignorant about."

"If anything, Mr. Mahoney was at fault. Aaron and Sophie didn't lower their voices to the benefit of anyone. He heard them. He heard, and he had the opportunity to teach his class something more valuable than multiplication and long division. Demonizing a group of people for the action of a few is wrong, and he should have said so. Instead, he chose to be silent.

When I look back on that day, I remember that—his silence."

"So that's what a teacher's supposed to do? Speak up?"

"I think that it should be a requirement. You never know what someone will take away from a situation. It was his job to serve as the positive role model. His silence validates the hate and fear that makes a Muslim ban and the discrimination against Arabs a reality."

"Can you tell me more about the discrimination that you've personally felt?"

"I'm the only Arab in the school, but it's different for me because my family's Christian, not Muslim. People see my darker skin and black hair and think foreign, but not necessarily Middle Eastern. I could and do pass as Greek. Plus, my name is Michael. The only indication of my ancestry is my last name, Abboud."

"There's no other significant event in your life that you want to share?"

"There's nothing else."

Rose peered out from the camera. "I thought we decided not to waste my time."

"We did."

"Then, don't lie to me. I know what happened with your father."

"Some things are private."

"If it makes you feel better, your Mom has approved."

I stood. "I'm done for today, Rose. I can see you out."

"I hear he's still in the hospital."

"I said I was done."

"You're going through a really hard time. I know. I get that, but I think you should talk about it."

"So you can record me making a fool out of myself?"

"So I can record your story, create awareness, and try t—"

"Who's listening to me, Rose? Even if you finish your project, who is going to listen? Why do we keep trying to educate people on things they don't want to know?"

"This isn't for them. Do this for yourself. I can see you're angry."

"You don't know anything about me."

"Because you won't let me. I included you in my project as a favor to your mother, but I need you to be honest with me and share your truth. I'm very close to walking out that door and leaving you here, but I won't do that because your mom is an amazing woman."

"The best."

"And she deserves the best from us."

I didn't say anything. I knew Rose was right.

"So don't do it for the racists, the apologists, or the ignorant people. Don't do this for me. Do it for your mom and maybe your dad. But you know, Michael?"

"What?"

"You would begin to heal if you just did this for yourself. There's so much evil in this world, it's easy to get lost in the anger and frustration. My purpose is to make sense of all these issues, and to do that, I need your story. I know why I'm here. Maybe you're here to talk and let go of the bitterness inside you."

I sat down.

She tucked her hair behind her ear and slid back behind the camera. "Ready when you are," she said.

I took a deep breath and willed my knees to stop shaking.

"My family has dealt with discrimination before, but never like what happened two weeks after President Trump's inauguration. Three white men broke into my dad's store on Madison Boulevard. He sells Ohio State merchandise. T-Shirts and branded cups, not something that should interest guys in their forties."

"We were eating lunch together like we usually do after church when the alarm system sent a text to my dad's phone. I wanted to go with him, but he told me to go home with my mom. My auntie and her husband were coming to stay for the weekend, and we still had to prepare the guest room."

My voice grew husky with emotion. "I wish I went with him. I wish he ignored the alarm. My parents are active members of our community. My mom serves on my school's parent teacher organization. My dad's in charge of the town's recycling committee, but that didn't matter. Not to them."

"My dad walked into his store, expecting a stray cat or dog. Instead, he gets jumped. My dad's an intellectual. He reads the New York Times on Sundays and teaches business courses at the university. He doesn't like sports. He doesn't like to run or sweat. He didn't know how to defend himself."

"They landed a few punches to his stomach and bruised his ribs. The doctor thinks they used a hard, metal object. My dad tried to run away. Instead, he fell and hit his head on the floor, and the cowards ran."

"After an hour of silence, my mom grew worried. She drove us to his store. I thought she was being dramatic. I imagined him in the back room, sorting through his inventory. When we arrived, the door was left ajar, and I swear there was something ominous in the air. When I saw him lying there, unconscious, I thought he was dead. I grabbed my mom when she began to falter as she sobbed. It was the scariest thing. We reached out to him. He was barely breathing. I don't remember calling 911. It's like I blinked and the police officers were already there, telling us to step away. I was so angry. He was my father? Didn't they know I had a right to be there? If my phone hadn't rung, I don't know what I would've done—probably punched someone. It was my uncle. They wanted to know why no one was answering the door."

"A few hours after he checked into the hospital, my dad had a stroke and slipped into a coma. He woke up three weeks ago, but he can barely talk and he'll be bedridden for the foreseeable future. I still wake up to hear my mom crying from her room."

"You know they graffitied the walls. After the police gave us clearance to go back into the shop, my uncle and I painted over phrases like, 'Muslims Go Home.' My first thought was, *but we're Christians*, and I was so ashamed of myself for thinking that because it shouldn't even matter. Those terrorists—and yes, I call them terrorists—violated us. I've stopped feeling guilty for being Arab because *I'm* not the problem."

The camera was still rolling.

"Do you feel better now that you've shared your story?"

"I'll feel better when my dad can walk again."

29

Michael Abboud

The door was unlocked when I entered the room, but Rose wasn't there. I picked the seat closest to the door so I was between Ndidi and Bianca, and then I opened my phone. Ignoring my messages, I went straight to Twitter, spending a few minutes scrolling through my timeline.

"I'm Ndidi56. Follow me." I looked up to see Ndidi peering over my shoulder. "I need more followers to hype up my blog," she said, as if that made sense, but I typed her handle into the search box anyway. I found her avatar. Her fingers made a peace sign, and her lips pouted for the camera.

"It's cute, but I'm thinking of changing it."

"Why's that."

"They say colleges look through your social media accounts, but you're a junior, right?" I nodded. "Lucky. You don't have to worry about that, then."

Mohammed walked to the door and opened it. "Where do you think she is? She's three minutes late."

"What was it you were saying in the car? 'We can't be late, Ndidi. It's disrespectful, Ndidi.' And look—she's not even here. We could have been to Starbucks and back by now."

Bianca glanced up from her book. "What are you

talking about? The nearest Starbucks is seven minutes away."

"Ndidi thinks speed limits are a suggestion." Mohammed slumped into his seat.

"Enough about me. Michael, tell me how the videotaping went with Rose."

"You had yours already?" I nodded to Bianca and asked her, "When's yours?"

"Not for a while," she said before returning to her book.

"Seriously, though, how was it?" Mohammed asked.

"She asked me questions about being a minority, and I answered them." I felt their eyes pressuring me to say more. "I can't tell you how it's going to be because each of our experiences are different. Just find a topic you want to talk about and speak. There's nothing complicated about it."

"Where did you guys meet?"

I responded to Mohammed. "She came to my house."

"Damn."

"What?"

"My mom will probably want me to clean."

"It's the hard knock life, I'm sure." Bianca turned a page in her book.

Before he could respond, Rose scrambled into the room. In her arms, she held her computer, the recorder, a notebook, and a drink. The cup had the patented Starbucks logo.

"That coffee smells divine. It's the caramel frappuccino, isn't it?"

"We'll stop for coffee next week," Mohammed whispered to Ndidi. He unfolded two pieces of paper and handed them to Rose "Here are our permission forms." When she collected them, he asked, "Can I schedule my interview for Tuesday at one?"

"That works." She took a seat and sipped her coffee. "I'm so sorry for the delay, but I'm here now, so let's get started. Now that we're familiar with each other, I think we'll feel more comfortable sharing aspects of our lives." She set her recorder next to her computer. "Identify your most important identity—gender, sexuality, race, whatever you want—and discuss what about it hinders and empowers you."

"Being black is secondary to being Igbo, my ethnic tribe. Everything I am comes from my culture. I love my language, food, and customs because they are specific to Igbo people." Ndidi began.

"What hinders you?" Rose asked.

"There's nothing about being Igbo that I don't like." Ndidi thought for a minute. "What I don't like is America's misconception about race and ethnicity. People use black and African-American interchangeably like they are the same thing, but they're not. Being black doesn't make you African-American."

"Would you say that you're African-American?" Bianca asked.

"No, I wouldn't. If anything, I'm Nigerian-American, but mostly, I'm Igbo."

"What about you?" She asked Mohammed.

"I'm black, African-American, black American. I don't care which one you use."

"So that is your most important identity?" Rose asked.

"I'm so many other things," Mohammed said. "I'm gay and agnostic but those aren't as visible. My skin color literally differentiates me from others, which—in itself—isn't a bad thing. What sucks is the racism I receive for being who I am. Like how security follows you around the store because the expectation is that because I'm black, I'm going to steal something."

Ndidi said, "When my brother asked for an application at a store a few years ago, the manager told him he wasn't hiring. When his white friend asked, the manager brought out an application. This happened just within twenty minutes apart from each other."

"People act so weird, too, like they're afraid of you. I remember being twelve or thirteen, running around in the park and this older white woman—she was probably twenty-five—crossed the street before I could pass her. I was so confused because she was walking more steps in the cold to get to her destination. It wasn't until a few minutes later that I realized it's because I'm a black boy and society tells white women like her that I'm a threat."

"It's funny because in the cover of the dark, they're so thirsty to be with a black man," Ndidi said. "They don't like black people on the whole, but they'll sleep with one to brag about to their friends."

"Makes me glad I'm gay," Mohammed quipped.

Bianca said, "I understand what you're saying, but neither of you have talked about how your wealth gives you benefits that other black people don't have."

"I never said it doesn't," Ndidi said.

"Of course, our class privilege benefits us, but what

does that have to do with Rose's question? She asked what identity is most important and how it hinders us."

"You talked about all the negatives without adding how your experience is invalidated because of your socio-economic status."

"That doesn't make sense," I said. "Nothing can invalidate *their* experience because it's their own. It doesn't get more real than that."

"I misspoke," she said. "I went to Eastbrook Catholic School as a scholarship student along with three other black kids in my neighborhood."

"Your point?" Ndidi asked.

"My point is that you experience the life of a white person. When you go home, you don't worry about what people in my community have to worry about. I'm sure in your neighborhood, there are no corner stores filled with alcohol and cigarettes. There's no poverty or gangs. You have the benefit of mentors and friends who speak like you. You don't get discriminated against for being 'ghetto', and your white friends can ignore your color because you all go vacationing in Europe and own summer houses in the same places."

"Where do you get off telling me what I do or do not experience?" Mohammed asked.

His voice was very loud. Rose was following the conversation. I waited for her to speak up and break the tension. She didn't. She continued to observe passively instead.

"And I resent the fact that you're equating poverty with blackness. I know it's against the stereotype, but black people do have the intellectual capability to gain economic power."

"You're putting words in my mouth."

"No," Ndidi said, "he's paraphrasing what you said."

"All I'm saying is that while you're black and experience racism, your life is not comparable to those who on top of being black are poor, too."

Rose chimed in. "Bianca, would you say that your most defining identity is your economic status?"

"Money is power. Everyone knows that. Being a Latina with dark brown skin, I know discrimination, but it's expounded by my lack of wealth. My scholarship paid for tuition and lunch; that was it. I was unable to pay for the dual credit and AP classes that they say guarantee acceptance to elite schools. I needed extra tutoring classes to understand the material because the school I had transferred from didn't have the funds to give me the tools I needed to succeed at Eastbrook. I was only able to pay for them because I started working. But once I started working, I didn't have enough time to study." Her eyes met Ndidi's and Mohammed's. "When you talk about race, you better follow it up with class privilege and how it benefits you."

"Michael," Rose called out, "I haven't heard much from you."

I found it hard to meet her eyes, so I turned my head. A glance at the clock showed there were ten minutes left of the session. I'd been hoping I could escape without having to contribute.

"I'd have to say that my most defining identity is..." My gender...my ethnicity...I wish she hadn't called on me. "It would probably be my faith." *Where did that come from*?

"Interesting. Explain this."

Well, since I already opened by big mouth, I decided to run with it.

"I'm a Christian, which surprises a lot of people. Everyone expects me to be Muslim. In school, the other kids would ask me questions like what's Ramadan or something like that. It was fun to pop their bubble by saying I'm a Maronite Catholic."

Only two minutes had passed, which meant I had to keep talking.

"Contrary to those evangelicals who love to boycott Starbucks, Christianity isn't under attack—at least not in America—and I hate that narrative. In this country, it's more dangerous to be Muslim or Sikh than a Christian. And to be honest, white, male so-called Christians create more terror than any other demographic."

"It really disgusts me how these Christians misrepresent my religion by oppressing minorities and women. These white supremacists use Christianity to justify every atrocity they've committed against humanity. Manifest destiny, conversions, slavery. There are so many other examples. Evangelicals support Donald Trump because of his Christian values. What's Christian about a Muslim ban or lessening people's coverage in Medicare or the horrible things he said about women? If you stand by Donald Trump, then I don't think it's God you're serving."

"I agree with everything you just said, and I'm not even religious," Bianca said.

"I do, too. It's so annoying to go to church and see all these people clutching their Bibles. Meanwhile, you hold the receipts of their Facebook post last night where they called blacks a violent race." Ndidi smiled. "I just love how defensive they get when you call them out for it."

"It's really disheartening. I don't question my faith, but I hate the community."

Ndidi shook her head. "You expect too much of them. Your natural thought is that they'll be good because they claim to be Christian, when you should assume that they're just as problematic as the rest."

Mohammed Wallace

"What movie are we going to see?" Michael walked with his hands shoved into his pocket. I walked in the middle, with my arm around Ndidi's neck. She popped the last bit of her Snickers into her mouth.

"I don't care," she said before throwing the wrapper into the trash can and entering the movie theatre.

"Still pouting?" She didn't respond. "Come on, Ndidi. We go to the mall all the time. Let's see a movie for a change, and I'll pay for all of us, how about that?"

Michael followed us inside. "I hear the new Marvel movie is good."

"Marvel is okay," Ndidi agreed, "but will we make it in time? It starts in fifteen minutes, and look at the line." She was right. The line stretched to the doorway. "We still have to get popcorn and slushies."

"You just had a Snickers bar, I'm sure you can last two hours."

"Never mind." She fished in her purse. "I think I have..." She pulled out a bag of *chin chin*. I rolled my eyes as she poured a few into Michael's palm. "It's called *chin chin*. It's a Nigerian delicacy."

"What is it?"

"Fried dough. It's really good." She offered some to me, and I swiped a few.

The line moved. We shuffled forward. The sound of Ndidi crunching *chin chin* softened the silence.

"Do you think the guy who picked up Bianca is her boyfriend?"

I glanced at Ndidi. "Why do you care?"

"I'm curious. She's so quiet; we hardly know her at all."

"After today, I don't want to know anything about her. How dare she explain black oppression to me?"

"I agree with her main point. So many of us upper-class blacks talk about racism without acknowledging our privilege. The way she said it left much to desire, though."

"Let's not talk about her," Michael said, "or anything to do with Rose and her documentary. Let's just watch the movie."

"I can help the next in line." The cashier waved us forward.

Ndidi asked for three adult tickets, while I reached for my wallet and pulled out a fifty.

"Your total will be $31.07."

I donated the change to the Save the Children charity, then our group headed to theatre number three.

"Hey, Mohammed, hold up." I turned to see my soccer teammate, Alec, almost jogging to reach me. Ndidi and Michael drifted toward the concessions area as I greeted him.

"What's up?" Alec Miller. He was loud, opinionated, and held mostly false beliefs. He also had this annoying tendency to start up a conversation with me as if we were friends.

"Why weren't you at practice today?"

"I already told coach I can't make it on Saturdays." I shrugged. "I have a thing."

"That sort of attitude is not going to get us to nationals this year. We're all making sacrifices."

"I'll see what I can do. See you later, man." I started to move away when he called my name again.

"You need something, Alec?"

"Actually, I do." I should've left.

"Coach is thinking about cutting Tyler and David."

His younger brother and cousin. I saw them play, and they sucked.

"I've heard rumors," I said.

He smiled like we were on the same page. "Well, a group of guys and I were talking about it, and we've decided to start a petition. We're hoping to get enough signatures to ban coach from doing it. So far, we have seventy-six."

"What are you protesting?"

"Reverse racism." *What?* "Hear me out, Mohammed. The school has a population of 750 students. Of that population, there are 735 white people and 15 black people. That means for one black student, there are around 49 white students."

"I understand math, too, Alec, but what does this have to do with soccer."

"If Tyler and David are kicked off the team, we'll have a higher proportion of black students on the team. We're protesting because that will disproportionately represent the black and white demographics." *What?*

"I know what you're thinking. I know that Octavian High does have a racist history and that we're trying to become more inclusive. What I—and many others—don't understand is why we have to end racism and discrimination to the detriment of white students."

"Tyler can't kick and David isn't fast enough to defend the ball. If you want your family to make the team, train them better."

"So you're not going to sign the petition."

"I honestly don't know how you got the nerve to ask me in the first place."

"The other guys didn't want me to ask you, but I thought I'd take the chance. You're always on our asses about how we should fight more for racial equality. I'm disappointed that you can't find it in yourself to care when whites are being targeted."

"Sorry for interrupting," Ndidi crept in between us, "but the movie's about to start."

Alec shook his head at me. "See you at practice, Mohammed. Bye, Ndidi."

"What was that about?"

"I think I was just accused of being racist."

She choked on her popcorn. "You're kidding."

"Apparently, the fact that the soccer team will have a percentage of black players higher than the black students that attend our school is reverse racism."

"No..."

"There's more. And since I refuse to take part in the petition, I'm allowing the discrimination against

41

whites."

"Let me guess, he doesn't see color."

"And all lives matter."

"There's only one race—the human race."

We laughed. "These people want to be oppressed so badly," I said. "How hard is it to practice and actually become a better player? Instead of rising above mediocrity, they eliminate competition."

"Just like a Caucasian." Michael shoved his hands into his pocket.

I looked at him for a moment. "That's exactly what it is."

Mohammed Wallace

Michael said it would be like a conversation. He didn't mention how disquieting it feels to have the camera's eyes on me. I put all that—the anxiety and fear—behind me and concentrated on what I needed to say.

"My family is from old money, as old as money can be for African Americans, considering all we've had to endure since being forcibly brought into this country. My great-grandfather was born in 1892. His name was Harold Wallace, and he was the youngest son of former slaves." I paused. "*Former slaves*. He was the son of former slaves. I hear this story so many times it's hard for me to grasp the significance. But that's the important part. In spite of his humble beginnings, he was able to amass vast wealth for himself in the Jim Crow era."

"His parents were sharecroppers from Georgia. They tilled their former owner's lands in exchange for food and shelter, but they didn't want that for their children. During the Civil War, my great-great-grandfather learned how to read as a soldier, and he made sure that each of his children could read, write, and count before they left home."

"People think that African-Americans are lazy and that we don't want to succeed, but what's more universal than wanting a better future for your kids?"

"My great-grandfather left home at fifteen. It was 1907, his parents were dead, and his siblings were all married. He was educated and had a head for numbers. From Georgia to Oklahoma, he held down a few different jobs, but it wasn't until a stranger gave him a ride to the Greenwood neighborhood of Tulsa, Oklahoma that he made his fortune. The year was now 1912. Oklahoma had just become a state five years before, and there was a massive oil reserve in the state. I think he knew when he got there that opportunity was in the air."

"It was two o'clock on a Friday when he walked into First Bank. He had the clothes on his back, a knapsack, and an apple. He walked up to the first person he saw, demanded to see the owner because he was an important prospective client from Chicago who could make it worth his while. He thought he was talking to a regular clerk. He didn't know that it was Elijah Lewis, the founder and owner, but I don't think knowing that would've swayed him."

"Harold Wallace had a certain charisma about himself. Elijah Lewis was a hard man, but I think Harold interested him. Elijah allowed himself to be persuaded into giving a job to this stranger, but over time, Harold proved himself to be a loyal, irreplaceable employee. That's when the Lewis family took Harold Wallace under their wing. They introduced him to the fine arts and promoted him within the bank. He was a regular visitor to their house, and in 1914, he married Hazel Lewis, their only child and sole heir."

"A month after the wedding, the Lewis and Wallace families pooled their assets to buy plots of land in the surrounding areas and stocks in budding companies.

After five years of successful business ventures, my great-grandparents left for New York with their two children. In ten years, my grandfather, Jameson, and their last child, would be born in Harlem."

"Harold and Hazel left Oklahoma with the expectation that my great-great-grandparents would join them in six years."

"It should have been a happily ever after—not just for my ancestors but for every black person living in Greenwood. White people wanted segregation, black people said okay. They started their own district, built houses and businesses, had black doctors, lawyers, and realtors. The schools were well-funded with dedicated teachers. It was Black Wall Street, and it was prospering."

"At a time when most grandparents were former slaves, black wealth was rising. Black people did that. Time and time again, under extreme adversity, we rise. And time and time again, white folks creep out from the woodwork to tear us down. Do you know what they did to Greenwood? Do you know why Little Africa, as it was called, is a remnant of history and not a living, breathing town still standing today? It's because white people did what they do best: looted and stole."

"They stole hope, lives, property, and black pride. On May 31 to June 1, 1921, Greenwood was attacked. They call it a race riot, when they deign to mention it, but I refuse to use that phrase. A race riot means that both sides were complicit aggressors when in actuality, we were victims of white aggression. They say the alleged assault of seventeen-year-old Sarah Page by nineteen-year-old Dick Rowland was the cause of the riot, but I don't believe that's true. Not when Sarah herself denied the claim. And especially not when I know that white people have a history of using any justification available to harm black folks. Just recently, Carolyn Bryant herself admitted that Emmett Till was innocent."

"But it doesn't matter what I believe or what the African-Americans of the time knew as fact. At the end of the day, a mob of angry whites murdered up to 300 black people. All those beautiful homes, hotels, grocery stores, and businesses were burned to the ground and looted, and government-sanctioned aircrafts dropped bombs from the sky. At the end of the massacre, the City of Tulsa arrested 6000 blacks, refusing their freedom unless a white person spoke on their behalf. In the end, 10,000 were left homeless. It only took sixteen hours."

"They say that we're lazy. Apparently, we don't care about education or want a better life for ourselves. We're hood rats whose only thought is on our next fix. They say all of that. Funny how they never talk about how white Tulsans refused to let African-Americans rebuild Greenwood so that we could never reach our former glory, or how the creation of Central Park purposefully displaced the 300 free blacks who lived on that land in 1857, or how Nixon led a smear campaign to make people associate heroin with blacks to criminalize us and destabilize our communities."

"Help the veterans, they say. But what about the African Americans denied access to the benefits of the G.I. bill, which was supposed to help veterans returning from World War I buy homes? They never talk about how banks refused to give loans to blacks, which prevented African-Americans from building generational wealth. Oh...I forgot. When you said veterans, you only meant the white ones because here in America, everything comes with the invisible disclaimer: for whites only. Tell me again how your ancestors worked their way up from nothing, and I'll remind you how their whiteness was the best privilege of all."

"When they think of thugs, they think of black people. They think it's funny to host ghetto-themed parties where girls show up pregnant and guys have Nerf guns that they pretend are automatics. They don't see color, but when they think of criminals, it's always about their fictional idea of a gangbanger in the South Side of Chicago. They forget to bring up Bernie Madoff and white collar criminals who steal futures with their greed and who nearly toppled the entire economy with this past recession."

"African-Americans are trying, but every time we see a *smidgen* of success, our communities are torn apart by the American government's intervention. The Black Panthers. They stood for community service. They provided meals for students, health clinics, and advocated for black pride. And hell, yes, they were armed because who else would protect black communities against brutal police violence? But surprise, surprise...the government had a problem with their guns. See, it's only whites who can retain their second amendment right. The smear campaign began—notice a pattern?—with the government claiming that The Black Panther movement was a militant hate group. The FBI swooped in. Soon, more than 300 members were arrested. Another point to whites, and lest we forget, the KKK is actively defended but Black Lives Matter is divisive."

"White America won. The Black Panther Party was dismantled. Blacks again knew their place. Martin Luther King Jr. and Malcolm X were assassinated. Mohammed Ali was discredited. Point. Point. Point— with a net total of zero for black people."

"I can keep going. Since America doesn't care to teach us about our history, my parents have taken it upon themselves to make sure that my brother and I know where we come from and what our people have been forced to survive. I know what you are all thinking. The Wallace family made it. How come all black people can't be like them. To these people, I say this: we are the exceptions. In a system of racism, there are success stories, but there can only be a few."

"Remember Tulsa and when you do, remember that no white Tulsan was charged with a single crime. A prosperous neighborhood was razed to the ground because blacks flew too high to the sun and whites were and have always been too willing to show us how racist they can be. Nothing has changed. George Zimmerman was acquitted just as the majority of police officers will probably be in the future because time and time again we are shown that our lives truly do not matter. At this point, we aren't discussing reparations, we just want to be left alone. Instead, we are vilified for not peacefully submitting to our systematic, government-sanctioned, and generational oppression."

"I can only be thankful that my great-grandparents were able to escape. What started from Harold Wallace's dream turned into a massive empire and wealth that my family enjoys today. I have money, and I love it. It gives me advantages and opportunities that I know most black Americans lack. Sometimes, I think the way I feel about my class privilege is the same way white people love their whiteness."

"It gets easy to delude myself into believing that racism is gone. When you can afford a house like mine, attend the schools and vacation in the countries I do, the black struggle may not always be a prominent struggle, but it's there, lurking in the wayside. I feel the same fear when I'm walking down the street and a police car cruises by. I'm a regular kid until the chapter on slavery comes and teacher and student alike peer at me, almost redressing me in the leather binds and loincloths shown in the picture. For a moment, I'll start to believe that I'm just like them. That's when they strike to remind me that a nigga is still a nigger no matter what's in your wallet."

"What about your great-great-grandparents?" Rose asked. "Did they survive?"

"They were never found." I stared into the camera's eye. "Tell me again how America's not racist."

Bianca Villamayor

My boyfriend was back. I smoothed pink lip gloss over my lips in a quick swipe.

"Bianca, I need to talk to you." I saw Juliet's reflection in the mirror. She was leaning against the doorframe.

"I can't right now." I dropped my phone and wallet into my bag and slung it over my shoulder.

She grabbed my arm before I could disappear out the door. "Can't your boyfriend wait? I need you right now. Two years ago, that would have meant something."

"Before I dropped out? Spare me the guilt trip."

"Fine. Have fun." I felt her hand leave my arm.

"Juliet...I—"

"No, you're busy. You don't have time for family anymore. Why did you even bother coming home?"

I watched her stalk to her room and shut the door. I stood in the doorway between the apartment and the stairs leading to the outside world. I jangled my keys in my hand. Did she really think I didn't care about her? I hovered by the doorway, never fully crossing over. I wanted to talk to her...I wanted to relearn the young woman she had grown to be while I was away. I wanted to stop fighting with my family and accept their love.

But Peter was waiting—and I had to go.

Bianca Villamayor

The clique had already formed. Mohammed, Ndidi, and Michael crowded around each other talking about the movie they watched this weekend. Rose stood in front of the room, rifling through her purse for the pen she lost. I was standing five feet away, yet I felt as if I were stranded on an island. I did have a novel in my bag and two more downloaded on my phone. I could whip out either and tune out the noise until the session would begin.

And then what? A whole summer wasted wallowing in anger and self-pity.

Before I could talk myself out of it, I headed over to their group. "Hey," I said. The mood dropped. Their smiles diminished and they shifted on their feet. It hurt a little. I didn't realize I was so unlikeable. I shrugged my shoulders as if it didn't bother me. "I came over here to apologize for what I said last session. I shouldn't have invalidated your experiences because of your wealth. I have no right, and I'm sorry."

Ndidi shrugged. "It's forgotten."

"No, it shouldn't be," I said. "I was out of line."

Mohammed said, "You're forgiven. Don't worry about it. I understand what you were trying to say, and you were right. Class privilege is just as important as race privilege." He nodded his head at the table. It was almost time for our session. The black recorder was already positioned in its spot in the middle. We took our seats.

As Michael scooted in his chair, he said, "That was a surprisingly good apology."

"Opposed to what?"

"You know how it is when someone says something offensive. They're all like, *I'm sorry you felt that way*, you know. They sound like pricks."

"Not to mention transparent," Ndidi said. "If you really are contrite, just say sorry and go. Anything else just screams I'm only here to maintain my brand."

"They do mean what they say. No one's forcing them to speak. They did that of their own volition, and it's obvious to everyone." Mohammed said. "It's actually quite funny to watch them try to walk back their statement. They start scrambling for words while you just sit there watching their foolishness."

Michael nodded. "It's their righteous anger that I can't stand. They get angry with you for being justifiably angry. They say, *you're twisting my words; I didn't say that.*"

"That argument works because the best deflectors don't say anything literally offensive. Instead, they use loaded phrases like the 'inner city,' which means poor, crime-ridden areas where the blacks and Hispanics live," I said.

Ndidi added, "Further equating poverty with brown and black people, and not only are we poor, but we're lawless as well."

"The dog whistling is prevalent everywhere in politics,"

I said.

"Don't tell me you're a political junkie," Mohammed said.

"My *MSNBC* lineup is Chris Matthews, Chris Hayes, Rachel Maddow, Lawrence O'Donnell, and then Brian Williams," I said. "I never miss an episode."

"If I weren't gay, I'd marry you."

"If I didn't have a boyfriend, I'd say yes."

Ndidi took a long sip from her coffee. "I'm a *CNN* type of girl."

We all looked to Michael. "*The New York Times* is enough for me."

Rose wrote down a few words in her notepad. When she lifted her head up, she said, "Would you guys say that you're politically aware."

Ndidi shrugged. "It's a spectrum. I'd say I'm in the middle, but someone like Mohammed and maybe Bianca are very involved."

"Do you think that teenagers in general are aware of social, political, and economic policies outside of what they have to know for social studies and history classes?" she asked.

"At thirteen, I wasn't actively seeking out information, and I didn't know many people who were. I knew the big things like Russia's annexation of Crimea or the Scottish independence referendum," Michael said. "But I wasn't tuned in, not like I am now."

"What changed for you?" Rose asked.

"I got older for one. I made a Twitter account at fifteen, and it made sense to automatically follow news sites like *The Guardian* or *Bloomberg*. I don't read every article, but I see the headlines. Social media makes it easier for you to be in the know. I wake up to a *CNN* notification each day."

Rose looked around the table. "Is Bianca's experience shared by you all?"

"For the most part," Ndidi said. "Maybe not at fifteen for everyone, but at sixteen or seventeen, life starts to get very serious. A lot of us are deciding which college we'll spend the next four years or whether we'll even go to college. And for some students, that decision comes with thousands of dollars in debt that will burden them for a very long time."

I said, "Many kids get their first job at that age. By eighteen, you're probably aware of how essential Planned Parenthood is."

"It can literally be the difference between life and death, and birth control is definitely not cheap," Ndidi said.

"You're thankful that Obama extended our health insurance coverage under our parents until age twenty-six," Michael said.

"Because there's no way in hell that you could add health insurance to your list of worries," I said.

"Look at the demographic here. Michael's the youngest at sixteen and Bianca's nineteen. What's happening on Capitol Hill isn't something we can ignore because each bill affects all of us in some way," Mohammed said.

"Like the Presidential election. I barely remember what was going on in 2008 and was only slightly aware in2012, but 2016 was different because I was different," Ndidi said. "I was older. I had my own opinions and thoughts on how government should work. And I knew that regardless who won, my life would ultimately change from that decision."

"We just didn't think it would change for the worse," Mohammed said.

Rose capped her pen. "Bianca, you mentioned dog whistling. Define that for us, please."

"The term comes from an actual dog whistle. You can blow it, but you can't hear it because humans can't identify noises at that frequency. In politics, a politician will make a statement that at face value, seems completely innocuous. A closer look, however, will easily reveal the racism, sexism, or intolerance. Remember when Donald Trump alluded that someone should use their Second Amendment right to bear guns and shoot Hillary Clinton?"

"It's never a direct insult," Mohammed said, "but enough is said to get the point across to the right people."

"For the past fifty years, the GOP has used it effectively," I said.

"Just follow Paul Ryan's political career." Ndidi shook her head. "The man is so spineless, I don't know how he can stand straight."

Mohammed adjusted a non-existent tie. In a fairly good imitation of Ryan's voice, he said, "I cannot in good conscience let Mr. Trump's wrongful words stand. Women are not to be objectified. They are human beings, and I'm appalled at Mr. Trump's allegations. My hope is that in the future, he will show women the respect they deserve."

He flashed a smarmy smile. "I don't really believe what I'm saying. According to my key analysts, this will ensure a national approval rating above 40 percent. Who actually cares about women? PC culture prevents me from saying what I really feel, but that's okay. I'll just help Trump win the presidency so that he can screw them over for me."

Ndidi laughed so hard, she almost choked on her drink.

"If that isn't Paul Ryan," I said.

"If that isn't The Republican Party," Michael corrected.

"The Republican dog whistle," I said. "It's an art form."

"We're not against transgender kids," Mohammed continued, with Ted Cruz's familiar Texas twang. "It's about a state's right to govern their bathrooms, not to invalidate transgender people's right to exist in public spaces. Think about the children."

"Like they did in Sandy Hook where twenty kids were shot dead?" Michael asked.

"Don't worry, Michael," I said. "Their prayers are with them."

"In the same breath, they legislate the removal of gun control laws," Michael said.

"It's true doublespeak, Orwellian edition," Ndidi said. "I'm not sure how they deal with the cognitive dissonance, but as you know, the devil protects his own."

"And they drag everyone down with them. Those literacy and property tests upper whites used to disenfranchise Hispanic and black voters didn't help poor whites, either," I said. "But then again, poor whites use their whiteness to further oppress black people and Hispanics, so you won't hear sympathy from me."

Michael nodded. "That's what makes me so angry. Defunding Planned Parenthood and getting rid of Obamacare affects them, too, yet they vote against their interests, you know, because liberals take away their guns and abortions are evil."

"White liberals are racist, too," Ndidi said. "Let's not forget those lovely northern abolitionists. They hated slavery, but did they believe in the social, economic, and political equality for blacks? No, they did not, and Abraham Lincoln didn't, either."

"The Emancipation Proclamation was a political tool that freed blacks from seceding slave states because he needed the extra soldiers to fight on the Union's side," Mohammed said.

"White liberals are the ones who pity me for being a poor African girl with no prior access to water, food, and electricity. When they travel to our countries, they go on safaris, refer to Africa as a country, and post pictures of orphans with heart emojis in the caption. They excuse imperialism, saying the civilization the west brought was better than our individual tribes' freedoms, and when you correct them for their mistake, tears sprout in Becky's eyes and the unspoken question is *why are you so mean*? They preach diversity, meanwhile their kids go to almost all white schools. They say black lives matter, but—and there's always a but—these protesters are too violent." She smiled. "They want to uplift us, but not to their level. They perpetuate the cycle of supplication so they can feel smug about their altruism. And if they heard me say this, they'd be the first to deny it."

"Not so different from the abolitionists," Mohammed said. "See how history repeats itself."

"Same story. Different time. At least they're predictable," Michael said.

"No." I shook my head. "They're just white."

Mohammed, Ndidi, and Michael shared a smile. "Just like a Caucasian."

I laughed. "I like that."

Mohammed Wallace

"You think she'll be mad?" Michael fidgeted with his seat belt.

"How can she?" Ndidi asked as she steered her Bentley into the parking lot. "We were in the neighborhood and developed a sudden hunger for Mexican food."

I stepped out of the car. "It's considered impolite to take up two spots."

"You have an awful lot to say for someone who doesn't even have their license."

"Guys, shh," Michael said. "We've been spotted."

I reached into the backseat, unbuckled the car seat, pulled out my brother, Kareem, and carried him on my shoulders.

"Come on guys," I said. "Let's play it cool."

Bianca's eyes followed us as the hostess, Juliet, seated us and supplied us with menus. I strapped Kareem into the high seat, studiously ignoring Bianca as she strode toward us.

"Juliet," she said, "I'll take it from here."

"But—"

"*Basta.*" She continued in quick Spanish. Five years of personal instruction, and I still couldn't understand a word. My mom would be so disappointed.

"How did you guys find this place?" She asked.

"Google search Bianca Villamayor, and this pops up on the third page," Michael said.

"I don't know whether to be flattered or slightly disturbed that I'm so easily tracked."

"Choose flattered," Ndidi said, "I always do."

"Well, you were our second choice. We were going to see a movie, but it was so poorly developed, we had to bail. It's a Saturday night. We're three red-blooded American kids. What to do, what to do," I said.

"I'll let you stay," she said, "I'll send Juliet with your drinks."

"Wait." I grabbed her arm. "Stay. Let's chat. Just the four of us with no video camera or recorder. The restaurant is empty, and it's only right to celebrate our almost-engagement."

"Right," she said. "If only you weren't gay."

"And you were single."

She laughed. "Okay, I'll do it, but not because you asked me to." She reached for Kareem. "I just have early onset baby fever." I scooted over, giving her room to sit.

Bianca Villamayor

It was nearing eleven thirty, which meant closing time. Ten minutes had passed since Ndidi honked goodbye, but I still sat at the table, staring at the special drinks selection. Mamá and Papá's soft Spanish wafted in from the kitchen. I heard Juliet laugh.

I used to start the party. I'd crank the radio up and spin Juliet around to the sound of reggaeton while our parents gossiped about our cousins from the other side of the family.

But I messed up. I messed up really badly.

So now I stayed at Peter's apartment and watched C-SPAN while he finished his psychology homework.

My phone lit up. Peter sent me a text. *You coming*, he asked me? In the kitchen, I heard 'La Bicicleta' by Carlos Vives and Shakira pour through the vents.

Not tonight, I sent back. I walked into the kitchen, instead. My family paused before smiling hesitantly.

"Why aren't you with Peter?" Juliet asked.

"What, I can't spend time with my family?" I grabbed her hand, twirling my arm so that she spun around in a circle. "Just like old times, right?"

Mohammed Wallace

"You never told us you were a model." Ndidi's hips leaned against the table. It was Saturday, which meant we were all holed up in the small conference room. After our dinner at *Casa de Villamayor*, Ndidi stalked Bianca's Instagram page. She called me when she saw a magazine dated 2014 with Bianca's face plastered on the cover.

Bianca hid her face with her hands and sunk down in her chair. "I never tell anyone I used to model."

"Why not?"

"Because after a while, I got tired of hearing, 'you're too smart to be a model.'"

"Isn't it funny how the people who know the least about you have the most to say?" Ndidi asked.

"As interesting as this conversation is," Rose interrupted, "I'm afraid it's time to begin. Anyone have a topic they'd like to introduce?"

"Let's continue with our topic," I said. "Ndidi brings up an interesting point about other people and their perceived perceptions about you."

"Not other people," Ndidi said. "Complete strangers will come up to me and try to correct me on my life experiences."

Rose tapped her pen against her cheek. "That's good,

but how does that correlate to our broader topic of race?"

After a pause, Ndidi spoke. "I've said this before, but when you're black in America, people automatically assume you're African-American. I can understand that. African-Americans make up a specific portion of the black demographic, but I still hate it. I'm Nigerian and American. Those are my two identities and my dual citizenships. It's annoying to be constantly corrected by people who don't know me and where I come from, as if they can tell me more about myself than I can."

"I've heard this argument before from my African-American friends. They say Africans think they're superior to them and that's why you guys want to separate yourselves from them," Bianca said.

"I would say that most Nigerians have a high sense of self. We love our culture, our language, our food. Between ourselves, we'll bemoan corruption, the bad economy, and the kidnappings, but with others, we put up a front. Everyone does it. It's the '*I can talk badly about my culture, but not with you,*' mentality."

"But would you say Nigerians feel superior to African-Americans," Bianca repeated.

"I can't speak for all Nigerians."

"Then, do *you* feel superior to African-Americans?"

"No, I don't. I just don't appreciate when my culture is erased because of this perception that black and African-American are equivalent." She looked at Bianca. "Some Hispanics are Peruvian, Bolivian, or Colombian. It's insulting to group all Spanish-speakers together as Mexicans, and it's an erasure of cultural differences."

Michael gestured to me. "What do you think of all this?"

"Me?" I asked. "I agree with her. Black is not a monolith; it's a race. Before I met Ndidi, I never thought about the concept, but as I got to know her, I realized that though we share the same skin color, our cultures are completely different. We speak different languages, we eat different foods. Our customs and way of dancing are different. I can't pinpoint the exact year that African-Americans became culturally different from mainland Africans, but it did happen. Slavery was horrible, yes, but I'm proud of what my people were able to accomplish. We were stolen, sold, and worked to death, but we're still here. Much of African-American culture is mainstream American culture. Though we don't always get credit, we create every popular dance craze. 'Stanky Leg,' 'Teach Me How to Dougie,' 'Juju on the Beat.' We did that. We dominate music and sports, and when you give us the opportunity to learn, we go far. Ruby Bridges. The six-year-old who braved rioters and protester just to go to school. African-Americans did that."

I glanced at Ndidi. "No offence to anyone, but I'm offended when people pretend like all blacks are the same. African-Americans turned a great tragedy into the greatest success by surviving and thriving in a country that still hates us. As much as I love connecting with Africans, you have to admit that they have benefited directly from the years we've committed toward the fight for racial equality."

"What do you guys think of all this division?" Michael asked. "There's black and white. African-American and African. Not to sound like a douche, but..."

"We're all humans?" Bianca finished.

"Yes, but not in the way the "All Lives Matter" group uses that rhetoric to try to silence minorities fighting for equal rights. What I'm asking is whether this separation does more harm than good."

"It's not a competition, simply variation. There's east coast and the west coast, football and baseball, the city and the country. How boring would it be if everything conformed to the same standards? Just chill and relax. Diversity is a good thing," I said.

Bianca agreed. "Not to mention, there's an actual difference between these groups. Take an Anglophone and a Hispanic. One speaks English, the other Spanish. It's not bad...just different."

"And not all ethnic groups are people of color. There are Serbians, Polish, and Greek peoples in America who still hold firm to their cultural and national identity," Ndidi said. "It's not just us. Everyone does it."

"White people who show appreciation for their culture are simply held in higher esteem than when we do it. They're not divisive. They're just *'in touch with their roots'*." I air-quoted the phrase.

"Not only that, but most white ethnic cultures are able to blend within the American culture fabric," Bianca said. "My family has been American ever since Mexico lost California to the United States in 1848, and people still treat us as though we're foreigners."

"That's because when they say American, they mean white," I said.

"I'm conflicted," she continued. "I'm proud of my

Mexican roots and my Spanish language, yet at the same time, I'm angry that I'm not seen as American as whites. My family pays taxes. We are community leaders, but at the end of the day, we're still foreign. It's almost like we're tainted."

"This is a real issue. Ted Cruz's father came to America in 1957, but you're the one who's told to go back to your country," Michael said.

"It's an effective way to cast us as 2nd class citizens." Ndidi said.

"To make us more believable scapegoats." Michael shrugged. "It's the American way."

Ndidi Ikemba

I didn't think she'd arrive so soon. When we hashed out the date and time for my interview, I did say Wednesday at three, but I didn't actually think she'd get here on time.

I rolled my eyes as the doorbell rang again. *I'm coming.* I just needed a quick look in the mirror. I swiped my eyelashes with mascara and readjusted my glasses on my face.

I hurried downstairs, throwing the door open before she could ring the doorbell again.

"Sorry for the delay. The intercom system is broken," I lied. "It took me awhile to hear the doorbell ring."

I picked up my bag from the floor and stuffed it in the closet before leading her to the living room. I gestured to the couch and left her to set up while I cleared the table. I almost sat down when I saw something bright red flash in my vision. I snagged my sweatshirt and shoved it underneath the seat cushion.

"Would you like something to drink?"

"No, I'm fine."

"Oh...well, I'll get some water for myself." I dashed into the kitchen, retrieved a glass, and filled it half-way. On the way back, I examined myself in the mirror. *Damn.* I should've worn my dark purple lipstick instead of the nude. I wondered if I had enough time to run upstairs and fix it. I faked a smile in the mirror again. The matte brown wasn't so bad, and it made my teeth look very white. I shrugged, picking up the water from the counter and headed back toward the living room.

"So, how does this go?"

"Just be normal. Act like this is a conversation. I might ask you a few questions, but I want the main speaker to be you."

"And I can talk about anything?"

"Anything that pertains to our greater topic at hand."

I thought for a minute, sifting through different words and phrases I wanted to include.

"I realized that I was black when I was ten—just three years after we moved to the United States. Of course, I've always known my skin is brown, but it never seemed to be a significant part of who I am. In Nigeria, I'm an Igbo girl from Anambra state. I have my ethnic language, dance, mythology, customs, and foods. In American, I'm just black. Full stop."

"In school, when teachers would take attendance, I hoped that when they got to my foreign name, Ndidi Ikemba, they'd stop and ask, 'Where are you from?' But when they'd pass through my name without even saying it, I'd get very sad because I had this desire to be known by something other than my color. The first chance I get, I'd tell the class that I'm Nigerian. Even though I was born in New York, I'm an Igbo girl through and through. I didn't want to be labeled as just black. I needed to be seen as different. I wanted them to understand my culture and origin just as I understood that Polish last names ended in -ski and Serbians used a j instead of a y."

"At seven, I couldn't articulate this, but at ten, when I realized that being black in America was a burden, I realized that the reason I wanted people to see me as different was so that I could escape the racism and prejudice that blacks—mostly African-Americans—face."

"And for years, I did escape the scrutiny. Being African has its perks. Americans think of us in a higher esteem for being immigrants who do well academically. They don't see our culture as ghetto but as exotic and fun."

"After a month at my new school, I found friends in this group of four girls. Within weeks we were sharing coloring pencils, passing notes to each other, and saving seats at lunch. One girl—her name is Melanie—had a birthday party. She was turning eight. After she cut the cake, her dad asked me which animal I liked the best: giraffe, zebra, or elephant."

"I was confused. I didn't even know what those were. He said, 'Well, haven't you seen them?' To me, this was a very ignorant question. I lived in Lagos, the most populous city in Africa. My estate in Victoria Island was twice as big as his, but for some reason, he thought I'd be the reincarnation of *The Lion King*. I was only seven, but I remember being very discomforted by that encounter. But then Melanie's mom passed me a chocolate slice, and I promptly forgot about it."

"When I was eight, my family took a trip to Six Flags. We were waiting in line for the Superman, and a white lady and her two kids were in front of us. She was yelling at them for throwing their cotton candy on the floor. She said, 'You shouldn't do that. There are starving kids in Africa. You should be grateful for what you have.'"

"When I heard that, I asked her, 'Who's starving in Africa.' I thought it would be someone I knew. She ignored me. I kept thinking of my friends Adetola and Helen, imagining their stomachs' rumbling. I kept asking her who it was, shouting off names. 'David? Bisola? Ebiere?' After a while, I think it dawned on her that *I* was African. She just rushed off with her kids. I started crying, inconsolable. I was convinced that one of my friends was sick, hungry, and alone. I begged my parents to take me back to Nigeria."

"After that incident, I wondered why people say the starving kids in Africa. Why not the starving kids in Europe or Australia. What about the thirteen million starving American kids? How come no one says anything about them? Then, I asked myself how come Africa is only brought into the equation when someone wants to use a negative example? The West talks about the corruption and famine, but no one ever talks about the hard work and laughter. If you ever go to Nigeria, go to a party. You eat, dance, have fun. We are warm, open people. How come in all the movies, Africans are seen as unsmiling militants who wield guns and steal? There is bad, yes, but why do you always stop there? Why not show the good as well?"

"Incidents kept piling. My friends used to ask me all the time for a picture of my hut. I got tired of telling people that the random black person over there wasn't my uncle, aunt, brother, sister etc. I stopped talking to Melanie and all the other girls. In fifth grade, I found the only other black person in my grade and started hanging out with him. He's still my best friend."

"I realized I was black at age ten. I also realized that blackness is not something I could take off. My foreign name and ethnic foods didn't and wouldn't hide me from the racism. At best, it would simply come in different forms."

Bianca Villamayor

I tightened the bandage that covered the burn on my finger. It was a physical reminder of why dad and Juliet did the cooking, and I cleaned tables.

When the clock's big hand edged closer to the hour, I said, "Is she going to be late again?"

The door opened. "No, Bianca, I'm not." Rose huffed in the doorway, hidden behind a dry erase board. We watched as she maneuvered the easel over the electrical cords to the front of the room. She waved off our offers to help.

"I'm fine," she said. "This won't take me long." She pitched her bag on the table, placing the recorder in its customary spot.

"What's all this?" Mohammed asked.

"I have a new topic I want to introduce to you guys."

"What if we already have topics picked out?" Ndidi asked.

Rose uncapped her marker. "I'll let you guys lead next week." Starting from the left, she began to write. "Today, the focus is on racism." She spun around, revealing the three words she'd written on the board: Prejudice, Discrimination, and Racism.

"Now," she said, "in our first session, we decided that there is racism in the United States, and in all the sessions since then, we've stated how it manifests in our lives, but we haven't yet gotten to the root of this issue. Racism is a word that carries a lot of weight. It evokes fear and anger, but what does it mean? Before we answer this, first we have to define prejudice." She tapped the marker against the word. "Who wants to start us off?"

The room lapsed into silence.

"Come on, guys. I know you all can speak. If I don't kick you out each week, you would sit here for hours talking." She placed her hands on her hips. "What is prejudice?"

"It's a negative feeling against something," I said.

"Usually someone," Ndidi said.

Michael added, "Mostly against a group of people."

"Can we take this further?" Rose asked.

"Your attitudes toward these people are based on stereotypes and preconceived notions. You don't have to meet a person from a specific group to have these assumptions, which means when someone does first encounter a targeted group, they see them through a muddied lens."

"Good," Rose said. "That's very good, Mohammed." She jotted down words onto the easel. *Preconceived notion. Stereotype. Negative.*

She moved on to the next column. "Discrimination. Go."

"Prejudice is the feeling," Ndidi said. "Discrimination is acting on the bias. I can hate...let's say, blue shoes. That would be prejudice. I'd be discriminating if I were to stop associating with people who own blue shoes."

I said, "The difference between racism and discrimination is that discrimination is acted upon on an individual level. Racism introduces the concept of power and how it is used to suppress. Ndidi hating and discriminating against those with blue shoes—while wrong—is a personal vendetta."

"Continue with this example and make a society racist against blue shoe owners."

"There are three sectors of society: political, social, and economic. In order to oppress a group, you need to overpower them with all three," Michael said.

"That's right," Mohammed agreed. "Politically, the empowered group can make laws to subjugate the lesser group. In this case, it's the Blue Shoe Owners."

"No, you have to start socially subjugating them in order to justify your political methods. You can start by saying that Blue Shoe Owners are savages. Because they're uncivilized, they deserve this unequal treatment. You demonize them. In time, people will wonder if they're actually human."

"Ndidi's right," I said. "You have to establish prejudice, and this misinformation has to be spread on a statewide level. First, we have scientists report that there's a biological and genetic difference between Blue Shoe Owners and the rest of the population. They're a mutative species."

"Cast them as scapegoats. If there's a drought, they're the reason. If there's economic hardship, put it on them. Eventually, people won't have to be told it's the Blue Shoe Owners' fault. Say there's a lack of jobs, all this preconditioning will lead people to think of the Blue Shoe Owners."

I continued, "Once the prejudice is there, the discrimination will follow. If people see a Blue Shoe Owner in the middle of the street, they spit at him, mock him, make his existence intolerable. They'll start to exclude them from public places. A prospective business owner will immediately toss out their application."

"That gives the economic racism," Michael said. "The inability to get a job because of who you are. Society can provide hard labor such as field or factory work that pays little to none, and the Blue Shoe Owners will have to take it because they have no other choice. The salary barely covers basic necessities like shelter, food, and water. Nothing's left over to invest in the future, ensuring that the next generation endures the same conditions."

"And what if there's a surplus of Blue Shoe Owners? Then, it wouldn't matter if they lived or died. Who cares if they get a livable wage? If one goes, another five can take their place," Ndidi said.

"Not only are they demonized, but they're expendable, as well," I said.

Mohammed said, "Some will find a way to remove their blue shoes. In order to endure in a society that hates them, they too will begin to side against the Blue Shoe Owners, deriding them just as they have been derided, denying other Blue Shoe Owners an opportunity to prosper."

"Then, there are the Blue Shoe Owners who have a lighter shade of blue than the norm. The racism they face is on a lesser scale than those darker than themselves. They'll want to preserve their privilege by breeding within themselves, uplifting their light tones, and discriminating against the dark ones, creating a culture of self-hate."

"Some dark Blue Shoe Owners will find a way out. Through creating a specialized niche, they'll brand themselves as something different to the non-Blue Shoe Owners to gain popularity."

"But they never have respect. They sell out their people by siding with the enemy and for what?" Ndidi asked.

"For a better life," Michael said. "For money and power. Even if it's just a smidgen of what the non Blue Shoe Owners have, it's better than what they would've had."

"Morale of the story," I said, "the system allows for individual success but prevents collective achievement."

"For everyone who made it, there's one thousand still living in drudgery," Ndidi said.

Michael said, "But we still haven't talked political racism."

"That's easy." Ndidi shrugged. "Make everything we said legal."

"You don't just legalize it. You encourage it," I said.

"It'll be a never-ending cycle," Michael said.

Mohammed finished, "That only a few can beat."

The dry erase board held a visual of our conversation. Rose moved toward the recorder to shut it off. "And that is racism explained."

Bianca Villamayor

"I really respect what you're doing, Rose. When I first started it was like whatever. I'll do what I need to do, then leave. But then I started to believe in this project. What we did last session was amazing."

"This project is only as good as the participants."

"The group really meshes well together."

"Well, I'm glad that you're glad. I thank you for the compliments, but—"

"Yes, I know. You're here to interview me."

"Think of it more like a conversation, or better yet, a monologue."

Since the beginning, I knew what I wanted to talk about. Now that I was here in the restaurant during closing hours with Rose's camera on me, I was frozen.

"Think about it for a minute. There's no rush," she said.

Breathe, Bianca.

"I used to model," I said and then laughed. "When I say it like that, the "*I used to model*," it feels like a lark. In reality, modelling was my life. I grew up on Tyra Banks' *America's Next Model*. I knew at five that *this* was what I wanted to do for the rest of my life. I guess you could say I scouted myself."

"My parents said I willed my body to grow to 5'9". Anything else was unacceptable. I'm naturally slim with a small frame, *gracias a Dios* for that. I wasn't too busty. With my catwalk and headshots, I thought I'd be the next Kate Moss. My dad was against it from the beginning. He'd look at the magazines and the light skinned women who'd grace them, and ask me, 'Why not become a businesswoman?' I'd look at my dark brown skin and curly, frizzy hair and ask him, 'Why not me? Why can't I be one of the first?'"

"I think he allowed my dream to persist because he never thought I'd make it. At the back of his mind was always the assumption that I would go on to college, get a degree in finance, and come home to work for the family restaurant." I laughed again. "When I was thirteen, Hollister put on a show in the downtown mall, and I walked for them. I wore a miniskirt and a pink tube top. In my wildest dreams, I never thought a representative from Ford Models Chicago would walk up to my mom and me and hand me her card. I never thought that three weeks later, I'd be signed to the company."

"For three years, I was jet setting with my mom to New York, Milan, Paris...taking pictures for Calvin Klein, L'Oreal, Urban Outfitters. I stuck to editorials. I didn't want to get trapped into commercial work. I kept a portion of what I was paid, sending the rest back home to help with my *abuela's* hospital bills. It was everything I imagined it to be."

"And then?" Rose asked.

"And then, it all went to hell. The money empowered me. I was sixteen, with thousands of dollars in the bank. My parents didn't let me waste it, so it was all just sitting there. I thought I was grown up. I thought that being financially independent was all there was to being an adult.

I thought that I could do it all on my own. An opportunity came for me to go to Paris and model. I'd be working more jobs, making more money, but my parents said no. They wanted me to finish high school. I didn't agree with their decision, so I pretended to refuse. When their backs were turned, I emailed my agent, saying that I changed my mind. She didn't ask questions; she just sent me my ticket and boarding pass. When my parents were sleeping, I left the house. I made sure to kiss my sister, Juliet, goodbye, and then I left."

"I was working hard. I was barely eating. The stress caused my hair to fall out, and I missed my family. I didn't realize how much emotional support they had given to me until it was gone. My agency put me in an apartment which I shared with nine other girls. We were all foreigners, living in France by ourselves at a very young age. I wasn't prepared for the parties or the suggestive men and sexual harassment. My parents had shielded me from so much, and then all of a sudden, I was on my own, trying to figure it all out. I was ready to quit, but I couldn't. I still had that desire to be the next brown girl with skin as dark as mud to break the glass ceiling."

"A year passed and then another, and my big break never came. I could have worked harder. I should have had a bigger social media presence. I know that. What bothers me is how the industry selected white models over more photogenic and better darker-skinned and Asian models. At first, I didn't want to bring up the race card. You're never rewarded for speaking your mind, but after a while, I couldn't help thinking that the only reason I didn't get as many callbacks as my housemates was because my skin color. Eventually, it became clear that my dark skin was the common denominator that stopped me from getting more opportunities."

"I was eighteen and seriously considering terminating my contract. Then, my agent called to tell me about a casting for a show called, *'Exploring Mexico.'* Finally, I thought, something I can do. I walked for the directors, brimming with confidence. For days, I waited for a confirmation phone call, but then a week passed with no new messages. How could this be? I called my agent, and she told me that they'd passed me over for a Brazilian girl with blond hair and pale skin. Apparently, I didn't fit their *aesthetic*."

"You'd think I would have figured I wasn't wanted at my first runway when the makeup artists didn't have makeup to match my skin. I guess I'm a hard learner, but if there's one thing about me, once I make my decision, I follow through. I quit the agency, packed my bags, and caught a plane home—to Ohio and my family."

"I worked at the restaurant while I studied for my GED." I raised my hands in subdued celebration. "Hurray for me...I got it. Now, I'm nineteen. This year, I'll be applying to colleges with my seventeen-year-old sister. My dream school is the University of Pennsylvania where I hope to study business at the Wharton school. It's ironic, but when I started working at the restaurant, I discovered that I do have a head for business. I want to use my skills to create a management company to help young models preserve and build their wealth."

"How was your homecoming?" she asked.

"I left home. I betrayed everyone's faith and trust in me. My parents were angry with me—justifiably so—but they took me back anyway. They supported me as I got back on my feet and figured out my next move. The hardest part wasn't dealing with their anger but my own. I was so disappointed with myself. Part of me wished I were still in Paris, fighting for my equal due while part of me wished I had never tried at all."

"Now what do you want?"

"I want to live a meaningful life. I want to build relationships, laugh and be goofy. I want to forgive myself."

From the corner of my eye, I saw my dad make his way to the back room. He waved at me. I gave him a small smile in return.

"Mostly," I said to Rose, "I want to be happy. The stress made me bitter. I want to release all of that and just...be happy."

Mohammed Wallace

"What do you think of this color?" Ndidi brought her fingers to my face. "Is it too dark?"

"They're fine."

"You didn't even look at them."

I held her wrist. "On second thought, I don't think that purple is your color at all."

She drew Kareem into her arms. "Your brother didn't mean to say that, Kareem. He's pouting because Tyler won't return his calls, and just like a man, he projects his anger out to women."

I flickered through the television channels. "You ever think I'm mad because you ate all of my grandmother's brownies?"

"You offered, so I ate."

"All of them. You ate all of them."

"How is your grandmother?"

"You're just trying to change the subject."

"I just want to know if she's well enough to make more brownies to shut you up."

"I believe that."

"But seriously, how is she?"

"Freaked out, mostly. How would you feel if a constant

barrage of death threats were sent to your mosque?"

"They're cowards. They hide behind words."

"Sometimes, words cause more harm than blows. I'm glad my family's agnostic. Imagine being black, Muslim, and gay."

"Triple threat."

"Literally."

I switched channels again. Queen Latifah's *Taxi* was on. We missed the beginning, but we've seen it so many times, it didn't matter.

"I started writing my blog, by the way. My first post will be up by tomorrow."

"You finally figured out what to say?"

She smiled. "It's going to be about racial relations. Go figure."

Ndidi Ikemba

It was our final session. My eyes slid toward Mohammed, Michael, Bianca, and then Rose, almost in shock. It seemed like yesterday I was pulling up to the curb with Mohammed for our first meeting, and now...summer was almost over.

School would start, and our lives would once again diverge. I sipped my caramel frappuccino. I felt maudlin just thinking about it.

A sense of anticipation was in the air. I could hear the seconds tick by, advancing closer and closer to the end of the hour.

Rose took a seat. "Before we begin, I want to thank you all for your contributions to my documentary. As I've already told Bianca, the story's only as good as the participants, and you guys are amazing. Each of you bring a valuable perspective to the table. You guys were respectful, mature, and cooperative. I've learned a lot from you and about your lives from our weekly sessions and our individual tapings. I want to thank you for honoring me with the privilege of seeing you in your complex and raw entirety, but not just that. Thank you for allowing the world to really see the diversity of human thought by participating in my project."

"Shucks, Rose, you're going to make me cry,"

Mohammed joked.

"What did we even do with our Saturdays before this?" Bianca asked. "I can't even remember."

"I know. This summer feels like it lasted a whole lifetime," I agreed.

"So what's our topic for today?" Bianca asked.

Rose shrugged. "Whatever you want. Does anyone want to start?" Michael's hand rose. "Okay, Michael, go."

"I was thinking about this last night, how Rose will edit and create the finished copy and publish it to the public, and as I thought about this, I was a little annoyed because I know what some of the reactions will be."

"Imagine us spending this summer in honest discussion about what it means to be a minority in America and having white people dismiss our experience and what we're saying as not true, as us victimizing ourselves, or whatever. This is supposed to clear the air, but I guarantee once the public sees this, there's going to be backlash claiming that we're instigating reverse racism."

"That always happens. Every time a minority mentions race or color, there's a group of people—usually white people—who try to silence the dialogue. That's been happening since forever. You can't expect people will change," Mohammed said.

"I'm not expecting people to change, I'm just irritated that people will invariably misconstrue what we're saying by painting it as an attack against white people. That's not what we did."

"This was about finding the truth and separating it from the lies," Ndidi said.

"Self-healing," Bianca said softly. "Forgiving yourself and the world."

"And hope and success and understanding ourselves," Ndidi said. "I decided to start writing. It'll be a blog about my identities: Nigerian, American, black, female. Talking about this conflict in ourselves that stems from being outliers was never something I did before, but it helped me understand. I'm going to blog about these issues so that I can further understand this world and...life, I guess."

Rose smiled, "You'll have to share the link."

Michael said, "This is what I'm talking about. We aren't victims too rattled to work hard and find success in life."

"It doesn't matter what people think of us, though, Michael, because we can't change that. People will have the same idea about you, an Arab, and me, a Hispanic, and Ndidi and Mohammed, two black people, whether or not they watch the film. What matters is that we control our voice and never let anyone speak for us."

I patted his head. "You worry too much, Michael. Smooth those wrinkles on your forehead. You're only sixteen."

"Stress will not help you. If you want to fight," Mohammed said, "then go to school, study hard."

"Be the Arab judge who fights undemocratic bills like the Muslim ban. Be that Arab teacher who raises a generation of empathetic, globally conscious kids. Refute xenophobia and racism. And when you do it, other Arabs will see you and aspire to do the same," Bianca said. "Create the positive cycle. That applies to all of us."

"Eventually, change will come and they will pinpoint it back to us," I finished.

Michael Abboud

I closed the door to the room and found the chair. I pulled it closer to the bed before unfastening the *New York Times* edition from my hands. I palmed the newspaper, easing out the crinkles. He loved the business section, so I began there. I took a quick glance at the hospital bed and the shrunken man lying in it.

"Ready, Dad?" I waited until I felt his hand grip mine in answer. Starting from the top, I read aloud, translating from English to Arabic as I went.

It almost felt like a regular Sunday afternoon.

I

My dad always called me his pretty little rose. I'd jump into his arms, and he'd swing me around. As I whooshed in the air, I'd laugh, feeling more secure than I ever could on solid ground. And then he'd say those words. "My pretty little rose."

When I remember him, I think of fun and laughter because there was always laughter when he was around. Sometimes, instead of driving me to school, he'd bypass the elementary, heading forty miles south toward the beach where he'd buy me ice cream and we'd let the water lick our toes. After my mother left for work, we'd roast marshmallows on the stove and eat them in our tents made of bedsheets and pillows.

I was never sad in his presence because he never yelled or was angry at me.

He was more a friend than a father. I'm guessing that's why he left.

When he did leave, he took all the laughter with him. It's like he packed it in his suitcase and it rode with him on the plane to his final destination.

I was six-years-old, too young to understand divorce, but old enough to know that my life had irrevocably changed.

My mom had never been the affectionate type. She was the taskmaster in my family, pushing me to do my homework and study. There were no spontaneous dance battles or food fights in the kitchen. She worked hard as a nurse to provide for us. She believed in two things: church and school. That meant I had to excel in both.

On weekdays, I was in the accelerated program, honors, and advanced classes. Saturdays were tutoring sessions, piano lessons, and SAT practices. On Sundays, we went to church.

In Glendale, Ohio, the only Baptist church was Salvation Ministry. Pastor Andrew Mortimer settled into town forty years ago with his wife and son. He started a Bible study in the Albright's shed and never looked back.

He tended his small flock with care. Every sermon was carefully modulated. He performed baptisms and marriage ceremonies with a gravity that silenced the crowd. His eyes were a celestial blue, a glimpse of heaven.

My mom was drawn to him because of his passion and commitment. He wasn't the kind to slip out into the darkness at half past three with a suitcase and our hearts. He was a real man.

We walked into the Salvation Ministry on a whim, the only black people to infiltrate a sea of white faces. I remember everyone staring, almost astonished. I was wearing my Sunday best: glossy, black shoes, tights, and a frilly, white dress. I clutched my mom's gloved hands, almost running to keep in time with her long strides. She ushered me into the second pew and set a notepad and pen on my lap—to take notes.

From his elevated height, Pastor Mortimer critiqued

the sinful world. The lustful, sexual urges of young people. The rise of drugs and loss of discipline of the American household. It was the devil's work, and we needed to beware. I left that sermon half-fearful that Jesus would descend at any moment to castigate the sinners of this world. As each spittle flew from his mouth and a vein popped on the side of his neck, I realized something. Pastor Andrew was a true man of God. He preached tolerance and caring, forgiveness and support. He believed that each one of us were deserving of unconditional love. His gait was staggered by his commitment to save the outside world and bring them into God's light. Never before had I witnessed such devotion.

Pastor Andrew didn't see color. He saw broken souls and communicated with angels.

Salvation Ministry latched onto us like a prize. After church, we were regularly invited to the communal gathering at the Pastor's house, where the adults continued in fellowship and the kids played tag in the yard and ran with the dogs. There were midweek cookouts with the Morrisons and Polawskis. I went to the summer camps where my white friends would always ask to play with my micro braids.

We were pulled deeply within the culture, molded and adapted, until we blended seamlessly within the church's fabric. Our evolution began with a small woman with greying hair. She wore it in tight curls around her face, and her name was Mrs. Motley.

She was a widow of ten years who had raised four kids of her own. Sylvia Motley had started attending Salvation Ministry since its opening and began teaching Sunday School only three days after that.

On our first day at Salvation, she ambled to our pew as the final hymnal rang and scoured through her purse until she found a Hershey's Kiss for me. Politeness forced my mom to allow me eat the candy. By the end of the service, Mrs. Motley had successfully introduced both of us to the fifty-two member congregation, Pastor Andrew, his wife, Cathy, and their three sons.

It was an onslaught of new faces and names and a new reality. We never went to church before my dad left. Dad would snore in the room next door, while my mom and I read our Bibles and prayed as one. We had to adjust to the culture shock, and the congregation had to adjust to us...but we made it easy by being the black people they never knew could exist.

We were not 'lazy, poor, loud, or *welfare queens*.' My mom worked hard, she kept the house clean, and I was respectful to my elders.

We were all brothers and sisters in Christ, singing hymns under the watchful eye of white Jesus.

...until Barack Obama became the 44th President of the United States.

11

It was never anything they said about us. They simply didn't like *him*. There was the rampant speculation that he was a Muslim, that he was foreign-born, and a terrorist. They couldn't trust him. Not him or his wife with her heathenish, sleeveless dresses. It was un-American, they said, and to them, the red, white, and blue of the flag represented a lesser god.

They never said what they truly felt: that he was too *black.*

I shrugged off the comments. They weren't directed at me. I was young, and politics didn't concern me. As the months dragged on, however, I noticed my mom's reticence to join church activities. She spent long stretches of time on Facebook, shaking her head at what had been posted on her timeline. I told her to take it easy. It wasn't personal, but she couldn't resist picking a fight with Mrs. Crawford arguing against the GOP. We couldn't go to the Polawski's dinner anymore, not since their daughter compared Michelle Obama to an ape. I answered worried phone calls with a vague, "She isn't home," and, "No, I don't know when she'll return," under my mom's watchful eyes.

There were a few times where I almost gave up the pretense. I never wanted to leave the church. Leaving the friends and bonds I had forged for almost a decade was as painful as when I realized that my dad would never be there to call me his pretty little rose again.

It took a few weeks for my mom to confront our pastor. She wore gloves and a little hat with a long dress and kitten heels. She sat ramrod straight in the chair in his study to regretfully announce that due to insurmountable differences, she was afraid that we would have to move on.

He pressed her for more, and it all came back. Every spiteful comment and wicked jab. Not only about the president but against the Hispanic couple who opened a convenience store across the street and the girl in the hijab who crossed the parking lot on her way to the local college. It was the intolerance and fear-mongering against outsiders. It was the culture, the environment of Salvation Ministry, a fixture as prominent as the cross hanging from the wall. It was the ever-prevailing whiteness that always exists and the subsequent superiority complex that followed.

And she couldn't—wouldn't—raise her child in this hotbed of pent up aggression and anger.

When she revealed all this to him, he was taken aback in complete astonishment. *He never knew.* He was ashamed of his flock. He couldn't believe it. Would it help if he was contrite, he asked her, but what were feelings without action? Somehow, someway, he had blocked his ears from hearing the evil within his own. For a man who spent hours lambasting sinners of the world, it was unsettling to see him silent when facing Satan within his very own pews.

It was very enlightening and sad in every way.

For all his faults, Pastor Andrew was a good man. It was beautiful to behold a man so good, heaven shone within his eyes. I used to think he was part angel and halfway into God's kingdom. I wonder though, had he been more firmly rooted to the ground, would he not have noticed the racism hiding in plain sight.

In the end, he showed himself to be a disappointment.

Afterwards, we began attending Trinity Baptist, walking in scant seconds before the sermon started and heading out immediately after the last *Amen*.

I I I

Breaking off with the church was hard, but it hit mom the hardest.

After dad left, the church had been her salvation. They were her friends and confidants who had watched me grow for the past eight years. But my mom wasn't one to wallow in self-pity. Within a few weeks, she applied to Ohio State University for her Masters of Science in Nursing. It was another hurdle to jump, and she invested all her energy to completing that one goal.

School sustained her. I was fueled by social activities. While my mom was with her study group, I snuck out to get tipsy before slipping back into my room.

And I kept in touch with my old Salvation Ministry friends—our parent's disagreement had nothing to do with us—while making new ones. I was the token black friend, but I mistook that for something cool. I couldn't dance, didn't listen to rap, hip hop, or R&B. Instead I spoke in the same accent as them, and was lovingly called their *homegirl*.

I felt like a translator, bridging the divide between the races. My experience as a black person was not my own. It was extrapolated to the general negro population. They'd see me and think *this* is how the blacks are, like we were a foreign species yet to be defined. Every action of mine, good and bad, represented the community as a whole.

In tenth grade, when I lashed out in anger at Mr. Parks, who gave me a B on a project when I deserved that A, I almost saw them scribbling in their notebooks, '*The subject shows signs of anger*'.

They didn't mean it as an offense, I was sure of it. It was subconscious, a side effect of being the only black girl in a segregated town. So I didn't let it bother me because what would my other recourse be...move?

I didn't analyze why it bothered me when Jessica told me that black people's hair doesn't grow. I looked at my short, kinky locks in the mirror, wondering if it was true. The Natural Hair Movement didn't exist then. There were no naturalistas there to tell me to protect my ends, that the LOC method was magic, and to stop using heat because I didn't need straight hair to be beautiful. I went to the prom with Maxwell Hunt even though I knew deep down that the only reason he took me was because he was fascinated by my thick body and bubble butt.

I ignored the micro aggressions until the truth revealed itself to me.

I V

"He shouldn't have been shot."

It was my freshman year at Ohio State University. After February 26, 2012, those were the only words that could pass through my lips.

"He was seventeen-years-old. He was buying an Arizona and Skittles. What was his crime?"

"You have to admit he looked suspicious..."

"Everyone knows you don't wear a hoodie..."

"It makes you look like a criminal..."

"Zimmerman was probably afraid for his life..."

I heard all these statements—and then some, and they all came from my four white best friends who just last weekend where salivating over Tyrone Price, the senior starter for the Buckeyes.

"You guys can't really believe that—can you?" But they did.

I called my mom that day and cried to her over the phone.

V

I pulled a disappearing act. I fielded calls and avoided my friends. In the first week, all of those irritations I suffered in silence as a child hit me in waves. I was drowning in a sea of ignorance, self-delusion, and shame. Scenes of my life played back like a story, and I'd shudder in disgust at myself for quieting my thoughts and allowing the racism to persist unchecked.

I was walking through north quad with my backpack hitched over my shoulders when I heard a voice call my name. I thought it would be Kelsey or Brittany, so I ducked my head. My feet touched the library steps when I felt a hand on my shoulder.

I took my earbuds off and turned around. "Professor Abboud..I'm sorry for running off like that. I didn't know it was you."

"I don't get to see you anymore now that you're not in my class," she said. "I just wanted to say hello."

"I loved Arabic, but I decided to take my film classes this semester."

"No matter," she said. "How are you, Rose."

"I'm fine."

"No, how *are* you—in light of the current climate?"

"Shocked." It was her silence that drew me to speak. She let me figure out what I wanted to say with no judgments or recriminations. "My mind is still stuck on Trayvon. That boy was seventeen, and now he's gone because of one man's irrational fear. I'm shocked about what happened, but even more so about people's reactions. There are debates going on in this campus whether or not he deserved to live. A black boy wears a hoodie out at night and his punishment is death? I don't understand it."

"That's the first thing you need to do—understand this. When I moved here from Lebanon with my husband during the civil war...I was so many things. Angry. Hurt. Tired. I came from a country with conflict to America, where there is still conflict. After 9/11, I faced discrimination and hate calls. Students began to drop my classes. And those feelings hit me again. I was so bitter."

"I was in the right, but what did that anger give me—other than premature wrinkles?" She laughed. "I spent all day arguing with my friends and my husband, showing them what these ignorant people were saying about people like us and reiterating why they were wrong. I wanted to know why they couldn't see the humanity in us? I was full of fire and ready responses, ready to match any slight that came my way."

"It was so exhausting to always be on the defense. I looked at my son and asked myself if I wanted him to be like me, always fighting and stressing? It is one thing to be socially aware, but it's another to allow yourself to be consumed with all that negativity. I didn't want that for him, and I didn't want that for myself anymore, either..."

"What did you do?"

"I took a step back. I needed to reevaluate my life,

cut out the people who made me feel bad or wrong. I needed some time for self-healing. At the base of it, I needed to understand myself and who I was."

"Life is so chaotic and changing. In order to save ourselves, we need to stay grounded in who we are and the things we value. I had to define what being an Arab woman in America meant. From what you told me before, you have not had the time or opportunity to do that for yourself. I think it will help. You don't have to forgive anyone...just make peace with yourself. You mentioned liking film, yes?"

"Yeah."

"Use that to document your feelings. Maybe you can track Zimmerman's trial. Unfortunately, I have to run to a meeting, but I want you to come talk to me. I don't want this to be something we talked about once but never executed. I'm free tomorrow at four. Will you be available?"

I nodded.

"I'll invite some other students I think you should know. We'll have snacks and drinks." She waved goodbye.

I had been tossed a life vest and began to float.

V I

What is my purpose for this documentary?

For a long time, I really didn't know.

I thought I did, but as the months dragged on, and I struggled to find my story, I realized that I had no theme.

Everyone needs their own way of understanding the world. It's not enough to wake up everyday and simply live. Our humanity demands more than that. We need to center ourselves in one unshakeable truth and keep holding on.

I didn't have that truth, and I wondered if there are others like me. As I began interviewing people to gain their perspective, I wondered if there were some special consequence from being black in America. And maybe not just black but an oppressed minority as well.

And there...my story was found.

Thanks for Reading

Hello Reader,

I hope you enjoyed Just Like a Caucasian. I would love to connect with you! Be sure to follow me on social media, and leave a review on Amazon as well. I appreciate your support.

Talk to you soon,

Nkem Odera O'Gonuwe

Nkem Odera O'Gonuwe

Social Media Platforms

Twitter: @nkemodera

Instagram: @nkemodera

ALSO BY ODERA O'GONUWE

SHORT STORIES:

Hera's Revenge
Mr. Smolinski
Mrs. Maman
Mr. Holden
This is Not Us

BOOKS:

Shattered, An After Ever Series Novel
Just Like a Caucasian
Akuko Iro

COMING SOON:

Seeking the Truth

**Odera O'Gonuwe's books can be found on Amazon.
All short stories can be found on her website.**

CELESTIA

DELU PRESS
DYER

ODERA O'GONUWE

The wall was built to keep people in, but all sixteen-year-old Celeste Navarie wants to do is escape. As the daughter to the First Citizen of Verium, her life is not her own. Celeste wants to be free. There is a world outside her city that she craves to discover.

In a turn of events, she is kidnapped and taken from the palace. Far away from her obligations, she has the opportunity to live the adventure she's always wanted.

But freedom comes with a price—a price Celeste might not be prepared to pay. Confronted with the truth about Verium, Celeste is forced to unlearn the lies she had been told since birth in her fight for the truth.

Celeste is forced to make a choice between familial loyalty and justice.

The decision has the power to decide her fate. Is she willing to face the consequences?

CHAPTER I

I fastened my hood tighter over my head, shielding myself from the bitter cold as well as discovery. I should leave, I told myself. Turn around, lock myself in the safety and security of my home, and never come back.

There were rumors about what happened outside the thick walls of my city. About the random murders and savage marauders. Most were truths. And yet, in spite of that, my feet propelled me forward, never straying from my premeditated path.

Plus, I had an appointment I needed to keep. I stopped. My feet stalled on the shallow snow.

"Jack, are you here?" I whispered. A three-tone whistle answered my call, and a grinning face stepped into my view. I greeted him with a mock scowl. "Did you bring it?"

"You have the money?"

My hands slipped to the collar of my fur overcoat. I flicked the button through the small slit and then started in on the next. I went through, unbuttoning the small buttons carefully and meticulously. When I finished, I parted the flap while keeping its twin clutched tightly against my shivering skin. Along the seam of the coat was a distinctive bulge.

"Don't I always?" I smiled inwardly as excitement replaced my anxiety.

His eyes roamed over the bulge speculatively. "How much do you have?"

"Enough to cover the cost."

He started toward the money. I wrapped the parted flap back around my body, tightening my grip on the coat.

"You know the rules, Jack. Open up." I nodded at the bag sagging against his feet.

"No small talk, huh? I can work with that." He grabbed his satchel. "Being a business-minded person myself, I appreciate that quality."

He slipped the leather straps free from the buckles and flipped over the flap that guarded the treasures inside. After pulling on gloves, he began to slowly remove age-stained documents from the satchel.

"You're in luck." He waved the papers around, fanning his grinning face. "I just unloaded these fresh from this morning's shipment.

"Careful," he said as he transferred the manuscripts from his hands to mine. The pristine whiteness of my gloves seemed unnatural against the yellowed sheets. My eyes skimmed over medieval English and my nose crinkled as I registered it as a political document. I hid my sigh. Literature, art, music. That's what I liked. Politics. I scoffed inwardly—if I wanted to learn more about politics, I only had to ask my father.

I gently placed the papers in one of the built-in folders of my cross-body briefcase. This time, I didn't hide my sigh as I slipped my hands inside my fur coat once again to extract the money to pay for the purchase. Such a waste, I thought. I wish I didn't have to pay for something so useless, but that was one of Jack's rules. No substitutions. Every present was a surprise, one I didn't know if I'd like or not until I saw it.

Jack has kept me here, dancing to his tune and paying his exorbitant prices, banking on the fact that I would never say no. He holds information, priceless information. Things he doesn't even care about.

This was all a monetary transaction to him. For me, this was love. And I wouldn't—couldn't—let him destroy invaluable artifacts when I knew I could stop it. Even if it were just a political document from medieval England. There was value in the words. So I would pay it, and I wouldn't complain because every month held anticipation for the big one, the grand novelty. I only had to wait thirty days. He was just lucky that this feeling kept me going through the many disappointments.

But, as of late, there had been more disappointments than successes. How much longer could this go on?

I should end this. But I wouldn't. Something kept me from doing so. Not *something*. It was the thrill. I lived on it. I waited for it. I marked my internal calendar every day, keeping an eye out for the haunted eighteenth. It was on that day of every month that

I stole from my home and left the sanctuary of the walls, willingly and voluntarily.

When I snuck from my room and crossed the steps from there to here, I felt just like a novel, like the heroine, plot, and words all smashed up into one being—one me—to create this extraordinary adventure. It's irrational, but I can't stop. I am an addict, hopelessly transfixed by the things that harm me the most.

The bad outweighed the good at every instance. I have been bled dry. For thirteen months, I've watched as the amount in my savings account depleted.

Like any good gambler, I saw the risks, but I paid no heed—to any of it. There was a cost to be paid for my misdeeds. I was sure of it, but as of right now, I've never had to pay the price. So it was with a certain smugness that I snuck from and returned to my city every eighteenth of every month, picked up the script of my life, and recommitted myself to the role that I was born to play.

I dragged down the zipper that lay in the interior of my coat where I knew the banknotes were hidden. "How much do I owe you?"

He smiled at me, shaking his head. "That's not all I've got for you, Celeste. I saved the best for last." He rummaged through his satchel until his hands pulled out a rectangular box covered with dull cloth and bound with twine.

My hands moved to touch it. "What's inside?"

"Just wait a minute." He shifted the box away from

my grasp, carefully unknotting the twine and pulling away the cloth. Moments later a book, not a box, was revealed.

My mouth formed a small 'o' in surprise. "What's the name of the book?"

"Why don't you figure that out yourself?" He tossed it to me.

My hands explored the cover. It was leathered and burgundy with subdued red tints. Gold leaf was braided around the border. The burnished lights twinkled against the contrasting silver moonlight. Two, long, rectangular halves met in the middle. They were joined by a gold, heart clasp. I fiddled with the keyhole that lay in the center of it then flipped the book around. The back was as hard, leathered, and burgundy, as the rest of it. I tapped my hand against the binding then met Jack's patient eyes.

"I think it's a journal," he offered.

"Yes. I figured, but where's the key?"

Jack snatched the journal from my hands. "I'm only selling the journal."

I glared at his right hand as it threw the journal up and let its slight weight somersault in the air. Such irreverence...

"That means you probably don't have it. Why would I pay for a locked journal?"

Jack let it spin in the air once more before holding it close to his chest. "I'm not here to negotiate, Celeste. As I've said before, no—"

"Substitutions," I cut him off. "Yes, I know."

He smiled. "Good."

I covered my face with my hands. I wish I could say no. I watched as he banged the journal against his thigh and flinched. I knew what was coming before I even opened my mouth. "How much?"

"Are you sure?" he asked. "It'll cost you."

I reached for the journal, itching to pull it from his disrespectful hands.

"I don't care. How much?"

"Five thousand citz."

I wrenched my hand back. "That's obscene. Five thousand...for a book? I've never paid more than one thousand for anything of yours, and even that one time was a stretch. I'll give you fifteen hundred, but I won't go higher than that."

"You know my rules, Celeste," he said as he carefully rewrapped the book with cloth and rebound it with twine. "No substitutions. No negotiations. Ever." The book disappeared inside his satchel, which found its way over his shoulder again.

I watched the book float out of my life. I saw images of Jack eating off of it, using it to swat flies, and finally trashing it. "Final offer." My voice was firm as I tried to imitate my father's commanding tone. "Two thousand. I can't go higher than that, Jack. You won't get a better price anywhere else."

"No deal," was all he said before he turned to walk away.

"What do you need this money for anyway, Jack?" I shouted after him as I stomped my feet towards him on the snowy ground. "I'm not here to fund your drug habits."

He spun around. Snow flurries flew around him in reaction to the motion. "As if you have a clean record," he sneered. "You have a lot of nerve calling me out. What would daddy say if he knew you were here with me? Don't forget that it was *you* who started this, not me."

"Yes, and it is *you* who has benefitted the most. You and I both know that I'm your best costumer. Who else would pay your ridiculous prices, if not for me? You need me."

"What I need is five thousand citz for this journal. If you can't provide me with that, then I'll find someone who will."

"Go and look. I'm sure you won't find anyone in this state willing to waste that much money. Take one more step, and we're through. I'm tired of being ripped off."

His cheeks burned red. "Hey, I only give you genuine pieces. I may not care about art, but I'm honest about my work. Everything I've given you has gone through all the proper channels with all the proper verifications."

"Because honor among street thugs is so high. Let's not pretend like your ways of getting your artifacts are in any way legitimate."

"What are you gonna do, snitch on me? I don't remember you being so righteous when you paid for them. Go ahead, Celeste. Do your worst. Go and tell your daddy that the big, bad street thug ripped you off. And while you're at it, tell him how many times you've breached the walls and—"

"Oh, stop it." My hands ruffled my bangs as they flew to my forehead. My fingers rubbed at the worry line etched between my brows. "Jack, I'm sorry, but all I'm saying is that the price is too high. I'd be careless not to be suspicious. You've never played it straight with the law before. How do I know that it's not me you're conning this time?"

His body turned into itself. He shoulders slumped, and his stance slackened. The lights in his clear, green eyes were snuffed. "I want out, Celeste. Out of this life. Out of poverty." He ran his fingers through his hair. "I can't be a smuggler forever. I can do better. I can be better. This is my guarantee."

I softened my voice. "I can help, Jack. I'll find you a job at the—"

His eyes turned hard. "I don't need charity. I need the money, for the journal and the document, which I've just remembered you haven't paid me for, yet. But don't worry about that one. I'll throw it in with the journal." He smiled and straightened. "Two for five thousand. It doesn't get much better than that, Celeste."

I laughed a little, but it was a dry and hoarse laugh. "I think I've finally learned how to say no." I shook my head. "This is too much, Jack. I can't keep doing this. Someday, we will get caught, and there will be hell to pay for you and for me. I just—"

My brows furrowed as my eyes caught a paper lying

west of Jack's battered boots.

"What is it, Celeste?" He turned, following my gaze.

"I just..." The words faded in the wind just as easily as the paper. I lunged forward to catch it before it whirled away and was lost forever. My hands grazed the paper before it was whisked away but failed to get a firm grip as the currents picked up, and the wind lifted it higher. "No..."

Jack stretched up to his full height and jumped. His body arched gracefully, and his long fingers plucked the paper from the air. I breathed in a sigh of relief and moved to his side. My eyes dropped, following the lure of the words.

It was a regular sheet of paper with normal margins and legible font. The moon shone down upon it, illuminating the piece from within—bringing an ethereal glow upon it. A big circle formed around the paper from the borrowed light in the disguise of an ellipse...or, a halo. Jack unfolded one of the creased corners and pressed it down with his fingertips until it lay flat. The oil-smudged pads of his fingers rubbed the paper's surface as he tried to chip away the brown grease-stain that streaked through the paper's area. My eyes worked to make sense of the computer-typed words that lay beneath.

Change is in the air. I know it is so. My mother tells me to be quiet, but I cannot stop this feeling inside me that tells me that something is wrong. We are a Christian people now and have been since the white evangelists came. We do not fall prey to the old juju that lies dormant in the framework of my village. But still, something is not right. I know it. Whether this feeling is from my Christian conscience or it is my ancestor's warning to me...I know all is lost, at least it will be very soon.

He knows I know, too. It is not something he has said or done, but it is a feeling. He laughs off my worries and scoffs at my pleas, all the while knowing that I am right. He jokes with my mother and cheers with my father and brings presents to my siblings. All the while, I know that it is a lie. He is a lie. And he is coming for me because I speculate the truth.

I am prepared to die young. I fear for my family, my culture, my land, and my people. I do not want everything to go with me, but I fear it will. The future is just so mystical. We try so hard to predict it, avoid it, change it. But it does not morph on the whims of insignificant humans. No, it laughs in our faces without breaking speed. The end is near and has been for a while. All we are left to do, all that we can do is wait, cry, scream, howl, pray, and then wait.

And so I wait. And I curse the fact that my days are numbered and that my end is near. It is the fault of my speculation. My curious mind. My transparent face. Because my laughs fall flat these days, and my eyes grow wary when he is near, he knows that I have guessed. And his uneasiness has let me know that my guess is truth.

Will he be able to look my parents in the eye when I am gone? Will he still give presents to my siblings? Will everything be the same or will grief beset my family forever? Will Chika still cry out my name in the dark even though I'll no longer be there to calm his nightmares? Or will his howl intensify with the loss of his sister?

I do not know. I do not wish to know the pain my family will feel in the coming future.

To be honest, a part of me is glad that I will be gone before the end comes. It is selfish of me, I know, but I cannot help it. I was not meant to take on this burden. I never asked for this knowledge. I am only fourteen. I am mature enough to accept my fate, but am I supposed to be superwoman, too? I've written this in the hopes that a part of me—the spiteful, fearless part of me—will survive.

Knowing comes with a price, a price that I will have to pay. But he will not bring me down because I have this, my voice. My truth is here for you to discover—if you choose.

Choose wisely if you dare.

As I've said, knowing comes with a price.

I peered into the words, seeing much more than simple, black type. It was the beginning of a story, a fairytale, an adventure. It was a possibility, and I had every inclination to explore this opportunity.

"I want it—the journal." The words escaped from

my lips unbidden, but with every passing second, they were truer. The excitement and thrill of the adventure rushed over me, reminding me why I returned every eighteenth. I came back for the sake of a new finding.

Today, I had come back for *this*.

I touched the paper, following the sentences line by line with my finger. I felt a connection through the confession. I felt as though I knew the person who'd written this.

Jack let me peel his fingers away from the excerpt and take it into my possession. He looked up, and his eyes squinted as if in a daze. "Evangelist? Juju? What are those words?"

Stories from the books I've read arose in my mind. The descriptive imagery created a vivid picture. Constantine. Charlemagne. The memories poured in, but I didn't share them with Jack. "They're things of the Old World, no doubt. Now, I want to buy the journal, Jack. I'll give you the five thousand citz. I won't even take the other document with it. One for five thousand, Jack. I'm sure it's a record-breaking sale."

His eyes glinted sharply. "You really want this journal, Celeste. So much so, you'd pay five thousand?" He shook his head. "A moment ago, you were shredding me to bits for the two for five offer. Now, you don't care"—he snapped his fingers—"just like that."

"Don't play games with me, Jack. I said I'll pay you, and I will."

"How?" he asked.

I waved my hand off abstractly into the distance. "I don't know, but I will. I'll get a loan or something. Ask for an advance on my allowance. Does it matter?"

"You'd be willing to do that," he said, his gloved hands hiding inside his satchel, "for this." I watched as he pulled out the dull cloth of the bound journal.

"In a week. I promise. On the twenty-fifth, we'll meet here. Same time. Same place. I promise," I repeated.

"Ten," he said. His face was stoic and hard, harder than I'd ever seen it. "I want ten thousand citz."

My feet stumbled backwards. "You can't do that, Jack. No substitutions. No negotiations. Remember? For you and for me."

He scratched his jaw. "Didn't I tell you that my rules are subject to change at any given time?" I shook my head. "No? How uncouth of me. If it's too much, then refuse. It's so easy, right? So what is it? Yes... no? Maybe? Come on, Celeste. Tell me. Tell me so that I can leave and get on with my life." His taunts swamped my ears. He flipped the journal up in the air and juggled it around and around to the rhythm of his dancing eyes.

"What happened to the honor among street thugs?"

He smiled grimly and caught the journal in one hand before placing it in his jacket pocket. "Poverty happened. But this, this journal, is my insurance. I can find another girl like you, Celeste, easy. There are hundreds of them waiting for a chance to mix up with a thug like me, all in the name of adventure. The choice is yours. This journal is yours, if you dare. Everything comes with a price."

"What about the price of friendship?"

"We were never that kind of friends."

"What? The ones who deal in honesty?"

"No. The ones who deal in lies. Let's not pretend that if you ever saw me in the walls of your fancy city that you'd greet me. No, I'm your dirty secret. Something that you feel smug about as you lay in your bed. I bet you wait for our nights together. It amuses you to court danger. The feeling keeps you going through your sad, staid life.

"Just as you do this for the thrill, I'm doing this for the money. I've never lied about that, and I won't start now." He strode toward me and rested his hands on my shoulders. "I want out, and I'll do whatever it takes."

I turned my cheek away from his face, away from his accusations, away from his truths. He read right through me. I felt as naive and childish as he made me sound.

Feeling like a novel. I rolled my eyes inwardly at myself. I was no more an adventuress than he was a gentleman. This was all messed up. He messed it up, and I let him. I'd known his nature since our first meeting. Only then, it delighted me to be acquainted with someone like him. Now, I fully regretted the times I blew my opportunities to end this.

But even knowing this, I still felt the pull of the journal as it drew in my soul. I wanted that journal. I wasn't prepared to give it up. I looked at the paper in my hand. To read this excerpt and not discover the full treasure would be a travesty, like glimpsing paradise but never arriving.

Our moonlit rendezvous were drawing to a close, and I needed one last adventure to keep me going past the next eighteenth and through the rest of my life.

I turned my face to meet his sharp eyes. A moment passed. And then another. The wind whipped and pelted my face with sharp stings and cold slaps. My hood was torn from my head by the powerful gusts' strength. My hair lapped around my ears and over my eyes, extending forward to tickle Jack's chin. The silver threads glinted in the moon's beam.

"I'll do it," I said, feeling his shock, and then his slow smile. The gambler inside of me lived for the thrill of high stakes vicariously through him. The hidden doubt. The exposed confidence. The raw victory. I felt it all as he experienced it. "I'll pay," I continued. "Just give me one week. And I'm taking the other document with me. Call it a parting gift from you to me."

A budding smile curved his lips. "I don't give freebies or extensions."

I kissed his cheek and whispered in his ear. "You do for me."

I turned my back on his bemused expression and ran the two miles to the walls. I felt an explosion of energy and the need to expel it. My feet swept past the small, rounded hills, kicking up clumps of snow, fresh from yesterday's storm. I maneuvered around the trees, ducking my head from the low branches as I swerved between the thick trunks.

Fifteen minutes later, I hunched over—heart pounding, chest constricting—with my hands resting on my knees. The wall loomed before me. It stood high, at least one hundred feet above ground, and its circumference stretched twice as wide. The smooth, stone, exterior proved to be un-scalable; it lacked foot-holes and hand-grips. I couldn't see it, but I knew there to be an interior, steel, framework. One slip, one breech, and you were toast, fried by the electric currents working underneath. True to its design, it faithfully kept outsiders out and my people in.

So much danger I put myself through. And for what?

My breath caught as I grazed the distinctive bulge in the seam of my overcoat, and then pulled out a slight rectangular box. It was covered with dull cloth and bound with twine. I carefully placed it into the built-in folder of my briefcase, next to the political document.

I peeled off my white gloves, stuffed them inside my pocket, and then studied my quick fingers in the dawning light. Jack would never let me get close to him again.

I passed the straps of my briefcase through the rusted buckles. It was dark and roughened from use. I swung it behind my back then rolled up my sleeves. My feet ambled around the start of the wall.

Moments later, I heard a hushed crack. I looked down. The broken remnants of a twig were left scattered under my foot. I looked beyond it. What seemed to be an animal's cache laid against the thick mortar of the wall. Slim sticks, tufts of snow, and thorny acorns were heaped in a pile. I knelt to the ground. My knees left tracks as my arms stretched toward the small stash. I pulled out the acorns and sticks. My arms swept aside the snow to reveal the underground tunnel. It was a gaping breach within the underground network of pure steel that shot about ten feet below the wall.

I pushed my bare forearms ahead of me as I lowered my knees and skid forward on my belly. I sucked in my stomach and slowed my small hiccups of breath as I squeezed myself through the seven feet of dry heat, musty air, and solid steel.

Somehow, I managed to smile as I made it through the tight space. I managed to grin as I passed by the artist's signature initials, C.N., near the end. I managed to laugh as my head broke through the opening, and I shoved the rest of my body out.

With a certain smugness, I stole through the night, unscathed and undetected. Letting the fading stars be my guide, I followed them as they led me to the palace, my home. I winded myself around the stairs and to my room. I collapsed on my silk sheets and feathered pillow. I gripped my briefcase close to my body and buried it underneath my fur coat.

The thrill was decreasing. I was left cold and tired, but an insistent thread of excitement persisted on beating strong.

That night, I smiled as I fell asleep.

an after ever series

DELU PRESS
DYER

ODERA O'GONUWE

One year has passed since Cinderella married her prince, but the time has come for the evil stepmother, Lady Rayne, to atone for her sins. She is judged and convicted guilty in the eyes of the court and the people. Banished from the kingdom, far away from all things familiar, she decides to take charge of her destiny. In her crusade for the truth she unweaves a web of dark secrets and harrowing deception spun by the princess at the helm of the mighty kingdom. Unwittingly, she fuels revolution, and leads a roar for change. Though, truth is on her side, the other forces refuse to capitulate, and the clashing sides fight until only one remains.

In the first novel of the After Ever series, the familiar story of Cinderella is turned on its head. Maybe the wicked stepmother is not so evil after all?

Chapter 1

"Is he here yet?" I asked as my arms pulled the curtain apart on the window before waiting for an answer. Outside, the birds sang across the clear, blue sky. Lush flowers tilted toward the sun to receive the light's blessings. It was a perfect summer day. Two years ago, I would have delighted in it. Today, the beauty is lost to me—along with every other feeling but anxiety, exhaustion, fear, and stress.

Behind me, Lucy, my housekeeper, nurse, and cook humphed. "You know how I feel about this visitor, Lena, but whether I like him or not, you staring out the window every five minutes will not hasten his arrival." Her eyes lifted from the clothes she was folding. "Here," she said, handing me a dull dress. "Fold this and relax."

I reached for the cloth. My arms creased the material mechanically in straight lines. All the while my mind recounted the events that had happened just three days ago: the trial, Ella's threat, my liberation. Again and again the words whirled in my head. They spun like a twirling baton, switching order and mixing letters until the world spun, and a jumbled mess of nonsense was formed; until the sun's light faded and Lucy's voice was drowned by the steady cascade of memories; until the seconds between then and now were erased. I was taken back to three days before...

* * * * *

It was an unbearably rainy day. Buckets of fat droplets stormed down from the heavens. Sloshes of watery mud on the roads. But no one was outside to notice the muck. They were inside, awaiting the sentence, and all heads were facing the front bench where Supreme Judge Wilborn sat perched at the helm. His voice, deep and pronounced, held the court under a spell. The spectators sat in rapt attention, ears alert, as he began.

"On the count of high treason to a member of the royal family..." My fingers grasped the edge of the defendant's box as the words reverberated in my ears. I closed my eyes, and my lips mouthed a frantic prayer. *Please, let me be innocent.* "I hereby sentence Lady Lena Ellis Rayne to life—in prison." My eyes flew open; they watched as Wilborn raised his gavel high and smashed it against the mantle. *No!*

My heart pounded against my chest keeping time with the echo of the gavel. *No! I am innocent!* I wanted to scream it to the rooftops and bring the blasted building down to the ground. Instead, I said nothing. I wiped my face blank of any emotion as two guards materialized by my side. I refused to let them know that they had defeated me. To let Her know that she had defeated me. The guards clasped my upper arms and dragged me toward the prison door, every step bringing me closer to my uncertain future.

I walked in time to their long strides when all I wanted to do was drop to the ground and kick them away. I wanted to strike each and every person we passed and wipe their faces of the gleaming smiles that said, *she got what she deserved.*

I knew what they whispered among themselves. They believed that the mighty Lady Rayne had finally been brought down low, back where she belonged, amid the trash of society. They knew nothing. It would take much more than a silly trial to defeat me. I will prevail. I will go home. I will see my family again. I thought the words so compellingly I almost convinced myself. Almost. But before I got my happily after ever, I would hunt down the woman who did this to me and... what? What could I do? I had nothing, and she had everything: money, power, the kingdom. I sighed. I would do nothing, and we both knew it. She had me backed into a corner; I couldn't escape.

How did I let it get this far? I should have run long, long ago, when the king first told me of my "supposed" crimes. I should have fled when he placed a guard on the outskirts of my cottage after kicking me out of Rayne Manor and depriving me of my inheritance. I should have left when there was no one to turn to. No one associates with a criminal. Even an innocent one. I had learned that the hard way. The truth was that I had had plenty of opportunities to escape, but I was too stubborn to take them. I never imagined it would get this far. Judge Wilborn's words echoed in my mind: "Life...in prison."

If only my old friends back home could see me now. They wouldn't believe who I'd become. Or maybe they would—no one would have thought that wild Lena could have caught a lord for a husband. The image of me locked and bound would seem appropriate. I had always been a little scamp.

Maybe I should tell the truth...

I ruthlessly crushed the whispering thought. Tell the truth? Who would believe me? Better yet, who would care?

Stuck in my thoughts, I didn't notice the flash of red shooting in the fringes until it exploded in our path. Our group stopped short. A woman, clothed in a crimson cloak, stood between us and the door. The guards made a swipe at her, but she anticipated their movement. Before their fists could connect, she pulled her hood down. Wisps of gleaming, yellow hair floated around her sweet face. The guards stood still for a moment, their jaws slack with disbelief, before they abruptly knelt. In a wave, beginning with the front row and rippling down south, every person knelt down and bowed—everyone but me.

I raised my brow at the intruder, ignoring the censure from our audience. The princess simply laughed at my disrespect.

"Lady Lena," she said, a smile curling her lips. "Come

with me." She waved at a guard to open the doors, and she walked down the hall, leaving me no choice but to follow.

I closed the door on my way out.

She led me to the first door on the right and then turned the lock. The princess slowly circled me, a small smile lifting the corners of her lips. "Hello, Lena," she said. "Aren't you glad to see me?"

I slipped into a belated curtsy. "About as glad as I am to see a snake, Your Majesty."

She laughed. "I think we can dispense with such formalities, Lena, don't you? I mean, you are family."

"Then, we should drop the false courtesy, Ella. We both know I was no stepmother to you."

"And yet my father left you all his riches, leaving nothing for his precious, only daughter." A bitter look crossed her face. "You didn't even love him."

I took a deep breath, ignoring the dig about my relationship with Edward. I married him for security at a time in my life when everything was in tatters around me. I was battered down with my burdens, and he offered me a life vest. Marrying him was the best I could do then, and I refused to let her make me feel guilty about it or my inheritance. And who is she to judge? From the rumors surrounding her and the prince, their hasty romance has quickly fizzled. I wonder if she ever loved him.

"You made your choices three years ago, Ella; so don't call yourself the poor victim," I said. "Your father was prepared to give you the world. You're the one who threw it away."

I still remembered how his sky-blue eyes, so much like hers, turned cloudy with tears and how his shoulders slumped when he realized she had run away. And when the grief passed, anger took its place. From that day on, she was no daughter of his.

This forgotten anger latched onto me as I looked at Edward's forgotten child. Not for the first time, I wished she had never come back. "You have everything you've ever wanted, Ella. Let me go." I poured a year's worth of stress into the plea. A mysterious twinkle appeared in her eyes. I looked away. I should have known better than to beg. I forgot that she fed on it— the vulnerabilities of her victims.

"Oh, Lena," she sing-sang. "I would, I really would, but this is too much fun."

"Are you happy now, Ella? Does ruining my life make you feel better?" My nose flared. "Tell me, when you first accused me, did you imagine the end would be like this, with me locked in prison—for life?"

She eased into a chair. "No, Lena, I didn't imagine it. This was simply an added bonus."

My deep resentment toward her bubbled in my chest, and my hands clenched at my sides. She taunted me with her eyes, and urged me to do something about it. With effort, I relaxed my palms. I kept my voice calm and steady. Only a hint of my ragged emotions showed through. "I can almost imagine it, you with your big, blue eyes, pouring tales of how your wicked stepmother mistreated you. I can see you kneeling at your husband's side telling him about how I treated you as a slave, making you fix my gowns, wait on my family, and cook our meals," I spat out.

Once again, I wondered at her audacity. How dare she say such things about me and ruin my life with those lies when we both knew I had done everything I could to make her feel included in the family!

"Did he strut around like a peacock when you told him that his proposal at the ball saved you from a lifetime of servitude?" I said, looking at her with fiery eyes.

She smiled. "What an impressive imagination you have, Lena. You missed your calling. You could have been a writer. There's more of a professional satisfaction from working for what you own instead of stealing it from trusting, old men, don't you think? Maybe next time around, you can change your ways, hmm?" Her eyes lingered over me mockingly. "And yes, he did strut around like the most unbecoming rooster. How insightful you are. Although, I must add, I did not kneel. I never beg." Her eyes seemed to say, *but you do.*

"Do you feel any guilt at all?"

She flashed her crooked smile. "Should I? I see this as a belated revenge. You had no right to steal my inheritance from me. Now, it is safe where it belongs—with me."

Anger left my body at once, exhaustion taking place. "Is that what this was about? I would have gladly given it to you, Ella. Was this necessary?" I spread my hands in the air, trying to grasp the agony this trial caused me with my fingers. "Why am I even here?" I didn't think I'd prefer the prison walls to anything, but I could not spend one more second with her.

She frowned. "Of course this was unnecessary, Lena. Didn't I just say I did this for my own enjoyment? As for why you're here, we'll get to that." She waved a hand. "Sit."

I did, but only because my legs were too tired to hold me up. The moment my bottom hit the chair, servants flooded the room, their hands filled with silver serving dishes covered in matching domes. They set the dishes on the desk and then whisked off the tops.

The smell of well-cooked chicken permeated the air, with hints of thyme, garlic, and rosemary. Cranberry sauce filled a bowl to the top; the succulent purple-reddish color made my stomach growl, reminding me that it was lunchtime. The tallest server of the bunch dished leafy, green salad into our bowls, adding a generous amount of dressing before bowing to each of us and setting it down. Ella dug cheerfully into the dish while I stared at my too-green leaves with distrust.

She laughed at my speculations. "Eat it, Lena. I didn't poison you." Her eyes darkened. "When I want to hurt you, you'll know it." She shoveled another forkful into her mouth. Tempted, but unsettled by her words, I pierced a leaf with my fork, inspecting the length of it before eating.

It was as good as it looked, maybe better. The

crunchy leaves left my stomach satisfied. Before I knew it, I had finished my first bowl and refilled it for seconds. In roughly half an hour, we ate our fill. The servers nodded and left, leaving with the silver serving dishes as silently as they came. I glanced at Ella before looking at the door. It seemed a bit contradictory to be eating lunch with her like we were the best of friends, or worse, the perfect family. My eyes snuck towards the door again. Maybe I could...

"Don't even think about it, Lena. You wouldn't take more than ten steps before you're caught."

"What do you want from me here?"

She took a long sip from her glass. "I'm getting to that." She set the glass down. "Earlier, I told you I sent you here for laughs. While that's true, there's nothing funny about actually sending you to jail," she shuddered, "with those dirty convicts. No, that doesn't do anything for me." She smiled. I was instantly suspicious. "Instead, I'm banishing you from the kingdom, effective immediately. In three days' time, I will send for a carriage to pick you up at your home. You will leave at the stroke of midnight."

I didn't know what to feel about her plan. Was exile better than imprisonment? If imprisoned, I had a plan. I meant to escape as quickly as I could with Drina, Stazia, and Lucy and flee to one of the other neighboring kingdoms: Brissenden of the North or Jenova of the South. With exile, I had no idea where she would send me, and I had no clue how long it would take to come back. My other plan was flimsy at best, but it was comforting to have a set strategy. Now, my security blanket had been ripped away, leaving me bereft and anxious. I wondered if that was her intention.

"You have nothing to say? Don't I get a 'Thank you, Your Majesty, for selflessly releasing you from jail'?" She pouted. "Lena, this ingratitude of yours just hurts."

I brought my eyes to her face. "Selflessly? Do you even know the meaning of the word? I don't trust you, Ella. I don't trust this convenient lifeline any more than I believe that you had a change of heart. You want something from me. I don't know what you want; I only know that it's something important, or else you would have easily thrown me to the dogs. So, what is it, Ella? What is my saving grace?"

She smiled her crooked smile, with the left side slightly wider than the right. "It's good you don't trust me, Lena. I certainly wouldn't if I were in your shoes." She leaned in. "The thing is, I was not asking for your trust. I was giving you an order; so now I'll give you a promise."

All amusement fled her face, and her cold, light eyes glittered as she spoke. "If in three days, you don't leave this kingdom at midnight in my carriage, you can be sure that I will hunt you down. I will start from every single person you have ever encountered in your life. I will make you pay." Her eyes flashed and her lips twisted. "I'll begin with that teacher who your darling Drina is so infatuated with, then your blacksmith, dressmaker, shoe fitter, Lucy, and on and on and on until I get you where it hurts: your family." My hands gripped the bottom of my seat. The bones in my shoulders were so stiff I feared they would crack. "I think I'll start with Drina. Do you think she'll cry out your name when my men steal her under the night stars?" My head started shaking frantically to and fro. "What do you think she'll do when she realizes you can't save her? Will she go limp in silent terror, or will she scream to the moon?" My body shook convulsively. "After I finish with her, I'll begin with your daughter. What's her name?" She tapped her finger against her chin. "Ah, St—"

I rose on unsteady feet. "Stop! I'll do it. Just please, stop." The last entreaty blew from my lips like the flimsiest whisper.

She smiled. "I knew you would see it my way." I blinked at her pearly, white teeth, my breath still falling rapidly. *Oh, how I hated her.*

* * * * *

Hours later, I was outside, and on my way home. My feet sloshed in the rain. The small droplets clung to my cloak, plastering it against my body. My hair was soaked and left hanging in front of my eyes, obscuring my sight. My skin was pelted with frigid drops, leaving me chilled to the bone. I had already walked for one hour straight, and I was still miles from home. Ella offered me a ride in her carriage, but I refused. I would eat a bowl of nails before accepting anything from her again.

Besides, the walk gave me time to think. How could I make the best of a horrible situation? I asked myself again, and like the other hundred times, I came up with the same answer. You can't. But I needed to, not only for me, but for my family. For their sakes, I had to try.

I could tell the truth. Again, the thought crossed my mind, but when I shut it down this time, I was softer and more regretful because more than ever, I wished I could. I wish I had told the truth to the prince before he married Ella and made the worst mistake of shackling himself to her forever. I wish I had told the king so he could have stopped marriage before it began. Before I gave her the power over me to do what she wanted with my life, I could have told the truth.

There was no use thinking of what might have, should have, or could have been. The fact is—it wasn't—and that was something I would simply have to live with.

To be truthful, even if I had the power to tell the prince or king, I wouldn't have. I never liked Ella—she was a spiteful, sulky child—and I never trusted that gleam in her eyes, but I never would have ruined her chances at a good match. Throughout my marriage to her father, I tried to love her. I really did, but she was so... evil. I was glad she married the prince because she was no longer my responsibility, and I no longer had to pretend.

I tightened my cloak around me as thunder rumbled in the distance and a lightning bolt sizzled in the air. A storm was brewing. It was distant for now, but it would soon reach me. I quickened my pace.

All at once, I became aware of a ricocheting careen of

wheels. A sleek, black carriage overtook me, blocking my path down the road. The door opened, and a young man with slender limbs crouched under the roof. He smiled, but it looked anything but genuine with the way his eyes flickered and lips twisted. He swept his arm toward the blanket-covered seats inside.

"Would you like a ride?" he asked. I made the slightest hesitation before a shower of rain poured on my head. He smirked. "You would definitely fare better with me than in an impending storm." He was right. I was soaked and had no other option. I squeezed the moisture from my hair before stepping inside.

I immediately moved toward the blankets, wrapping them around my body tightly, letting no heat escape. I fidgeted with the cloth for a while trying to find a nice position when I became aware of silver eyes staring at me. He smiled. "Comfortable?"

I adjusted the folds one last time. "Yes," I said, raising my chin. "I am."

We sat in silence for a few moments until he broke it with his question, "Do you have an address?"

I blinked once before rattling off directions to the outskirts of my village. From there, I could walk the rest of the way to my cottage. "I hope it's not too far out of the way."

"It is, but it's a pleasant diversion." He nodded at me and then picked up a notebook and started writing.

I turned toward the window seeing none of the scenery. I was making a mental checklist for when I got home. I needed to pack, of course. Lucy could help me with that. Then, I needed to make arrangements for my girls. I didn't trust our neighbors or Ella enough to leave them alone with Lucy, but who could I trust them with? I had a short list of friends, but after so many years of silence between us, would they help me? I sighed, adding another item to my list of regrets.

The carriage stilled to a halt with an easy grace. I looked out the window and frowned. This was not the address I gave him. I opened my mouth in protest when he grabbed my arm and jerked me up. "What are you doing?" I tried yanking my arm from his grasp. His hand tightened its grip.

He kicked the door open with his foot. "Don't worry, Lady Rayne. I won't harm a hair on your head. I just want to have a little chat."

I didn't listen to him. I screamed. My voice became shriller as each second passed, but he didn't slow down. He chuckled. "Don't even bother. The men around here ignore such cries for help. All that screaming would only irritate them."

At his words, I glanced at my surroundings for the first time. The air was tinged with the foul scent of gin and sweat. The grass was brown, and the buildings were shacks, poorly constructed from wood and nails. The people looked even worse. They loitered at the sides of the walls, a layer of filth on their weathered skin. Involuntarily, I leaned against my captor. "What do you want from me?"

He led us to a building holding itself together slightly better than the rest. "Just to talk." I didn't believe him.

"We could have talked in the carriage." I watched as the bouncer nodded to him and opened the door wide enough for us to pass. I looked at him again. He didn't seem like the type who would rumble with such ruffians.

His clothes were well-cut, showing his long limbs to perfection. His hair was a bit too long, brushing against his shoulders, but it was groomed. And no one here could have afforded his carriage. Yet, there was a certain air of danger around him, skulking in his twisted smile and bright eyes. It was barely there, but it was enough.

He ignored me, holding a conversation with the bartender. Five minutes passed before he turned back to me. "What do you want to drink?"

My eyes widened. "Oh, so you do remember I exist. And here I was beginning to think I was part of the furniture." He ignored me again, ordering water for me instead. He took our drinks with one hand and led us to a table on the second level, far away from the other customers.

I took a deep breath. "Okay, you have my attention now. What was so important that you had to steal me from the road and bring me to this bar?" I paused. Then, I narrowed my eyes, remembering what he said outside. "And how did you know my name?" I stood up. "Who are you?"

"Sit down," he said. "I brought you for a private conversation, not to attract attention."

I remained standing. "I don't see how we can have a private conversation when I don't even know your name." I shook my head. "Why I stayed so long with you is a mystery to me, too." I headed towards the doors.

"Wait." He shot up as quickly as lightning. His eyes peered into mine, earnest and serious. "You might want to stay a while." Seeing my disbelief, he went on. "I have information you might want—about the trial... and Princess Ella." His voice dropped to a whisper.

I swallowed. "What do you know?"

He nodded at the table. "Sit." This time, I did. He sat across from me, downing half his drink in one gulp and then looked at me.

"Do you know how many people have been tried for treason in the past year, Lady Rayne?" His eyes stared into mine until I answered his question with a shrug. "A little less than fifty—that's more than there has ever been since the Great War." His brows lifted expressively.

"Now, of that fifty, how many of them do you suppose were put to death or imprisoned?" Again, I lifted my shoulders. "Almost all of them," he said. He leaned back in his seat and swirled his glass in one hand. His lips lifted in a half-smile, and his eyes sharpened.

"Now, I've seen a lot of things in my life, crazy, inexplicable things—most of which come from my profession. But never have I, up until today, seen a woman charged with the highest offense in the kingdom..." Those stark, grey eyes cut through mine while the ever-present half-smile played at his mouth. "... released from prison." He finished his drink and then set the glass down with a clang.

We sat in silence while the barmaid refilled his glass, tossing him a saucy smile before leaving.

I lifted my elbows and set them on the edge of the table. "What does that have to do with Princess Ella?" I studied him hard, changing my opinion of him once again. Now, I could tell how he could easily associate with the thugs in this quarter. Before, the image was barely a glimmer. Now, the picture was vivid and lurid with detail.

The easy grace about him didn't suggest a gentleman's background like I thought. No, it was like the manipulative slowness of a snake. His lithe limbs and those eyes only enhanced the likeness.

In that sense, he was worse than the small-minded men here. From them, one got what one expected—petty theft and careless murders. He would bring a level of sophistication to the slaying of his opponent, something utterly unexpected yet completely in character. Bringing me here to the slums was no mistake. He wanted me to see the comparisons between them and him.

"Oh, Lady Rayne, you stole my line." He smiled. "I'll ignore that question and pretend that you didn't crush my opening salvo." He cleared his throat, his features taking on an exaggerated twist. "Now, I know what you're thinking. What does this have to do with Princess Ella, you ask?" He wagged his brows, smiling wider when he saw me trying to stifle a snort. I had to remember to add jester to the list... along with mysterious rogue and kidnapper.

All too soon, his face fell. All comedy swept from his expression, and the mask was back. "As I said earlier, in my profession, you see all sorts of things." He chuckled, but it lacked mirth. "You also meet all kinds of people, but never have I ever met someone like Princess Ella."

I gasped, looking around at the other customers before turning back to him.

"Have you lost your mind?" I asked. My heart still pounded against my chest. "Keep your voice down. People disappear for saying less than that."

He smiled mockingly. "No one here cares about that. Only two thoughts cloud their mind—gin and women. Anything more is lost to them." His eyes roamed the sea of drinking men. Those sharp, grey orbs sorted who was drunk and who was not quite far behind.

He snorted derisively at the flirtatious interactions between the men and the serving girls. The women would swing their hips with a vivacious roll, angling for a bigger tip, all the while, avoiding greedy hands.

He was right. No one cared about us.

He shrugged. "Besides, most of the lot down there," he nodded at the first level, "are easterners, and you and I both know how bitter their feelings are towards the west and how little they care about the royals."

I nodded my head in comprehension, but still added, "You can never be too careful. The walls have ears all over this kingdom, and I have no wish to be dragged into another trial right after ending one."

His back stiffened. "You, of all people, have to know that I'm right. The people adore her. Everyone sings praises of the paragon princess, but I see how cold that smile is and how sterile her big, blue eyes are. I see her." His mask slipped, and his eyes showed a well of incredible sadness; I knew he spoke from experience.

For a brief moment, he was locked in his personal torment.

I blinked once, and the mask was back. "I don't have any real evidence," he said, "but I know she's up to something. Call it intuition." He turned to me. The wheels churned in my head. I could see where this was going.

"You want me to help you. Why?"

I expected some drawn-out explanation, detailing all the reasons I should join his cause. After listening, I imagined turning down each and every one of them. He wouldn't accept my refusal—not at first—but after begging and pleading, he would give up and take me home where I would wait until Ella fetched me, and then I would find a way to escape.

But what he said next completely contradicted my expectations.

"Because," he said, "out of all the people the dragon has captured, it has spared one, and I want to know why."

I was disarmed by this simple statement. I waited for him to say more. When he didn't, I found that I couldn't say no. I wanted to know why, too, and I couldn't do it on my own.

"I need some time to think," I said, still turning this new thread in my mind. "I'll give you my answer in three days."

He nodded, pushing himself up to his feet. "Then, I'll see you in three days." He reached into his pocket and pulled a card out. "I have another engagement;

will give directions for the carriage to drop you at home." He dropped the card on the table. "I'll be in touch." He nodded his goodbye.

My eyebrows furrowed as I read the card:

Ambrose Duvall
PRIVATE INVESTIGATOR

"I'll see you in three days, Ambrose Duvall, private investigator?" I looked up at him with an inquiring brow.

A shy smile crossed his lips. He shook his head once and then left. I sat back, sipping my untouched water, digesting what he said.

I was a forward-thinking person until recently. I used to shut my eyes from my past and think only of the future.

But, his description of Ella brought back the image of a carriage rolling on black tar, carrying the occupants toward a towering castle on a hilltop.

When it rolled to a stop, the man opened the door and helped his lady down the steps, holding her hand. Her feet first touched the ground when a beautiful, young girl flew down the wide staircase from the castle. Her yellow hair streamed in the sunlight and her blue eyes smiled. She raced to her father heedlessly, drawing to a stop when she saw his hand on another woman. Her brow furrowed as her father introduced them.

"Ella, my darling," he said. "I know you wanted a new ball gown, but I brought you something much

better." He cradled his daughter's chin in his hands and kissed her forehead before pulling the other woman forward. "This is Lady Lena Rayne, your new mother."

Ella stared with incomprehension at the newcomer before her gaze was captured by a nurse alighting from the carriage, an infant in one arm, and a young girl hiding behind Lady Lena's skirts.

The man smiled at them. He nodded at the girl. "This is Miss Drina Pallon." His eyes flicked to the cherubic bundle in the nurse's arms. "And that is Miss Stazia Ellis. Your new sisters." He rubbed his hands together. "I hope you aren't too disappointed, my dear." All eyes were on her, anticipating a reaction.

She smiled, kissed her father noisily on the cheek, and then grasped her new stepmother in a tight hug. "We're going to get along famously, Mother." The words were said in a sweet song and a smile tinged her lips, but her eyes were a cold, cold blue. And her stepmother felt chills, slow waves that began at the tip of her fingertips and ran through her body until they touched her toes.

"Yes," the stepmother said faintly in answer. "I hope we do."

ABOUT THE AUTHOR

Nkem Odera O'Gonuwe is an 18 year old who lives in the Midwest. She's been writing since she was 2 years old and has been published since 2015. She's currently studying Informatics. She hopes to one day be a successful tech entrepreneur while holding an illustrious writing career.

Visit Odera's Website to keep updated:
www.oderawrites.com

Made in the USA
Middletown, DE
03 January 2019